I expect the most interesting event that whole Sunday was when Miss Sarah took her bonnet off. She kept it on as long as she could, saying she didn't want to go inside on such a fine day and couldn't she just walk out and see my crops and the barn and the livestock and all? It was an uncommon thing for a woman to want, but I just laid it to her being an uncommon woman and thought no more about it. I was ready to start right off with her, but Miss Patience gave Miss Sarah a quick little scowl and shook her head a mite, and Miss Sarah sighed and came on inside. It was for all the world like you see husbands and wives do. Then my wife started saying, like women do, "Lay off your wraps now, be comfortable now," and Miss Patience gave Miss Sarah a little nod. At first Miss Sarah looked worried, but then she shrugged and laid her bonnet off.

And there she stood with about as much hair on her as the preacher, just enough of it to make a tail tied up behind and not what you'd call a long tail at that.

My wife blurts out, "Why, where's your hair?"

"It went," Miss Sarah says.

BOOKS BY ISABEL MILLER

Patience and Sarah
*The Love of Good Women**
*Side by Side**
*A Dooryard Full of Flowers**

*Published by The Naiad Press, Inc.

ISABEL MILLER

A DOORYARD FULL OF FLOWERS

AND OTHER SHORT PIECES

The Naiad Press, Inc.
1993
JACKSON COUNTY LIBRARY SERVICES
MEDFORD OREGON 97501

Printed in the United States of America on acid-free paper
First Edition

Edited by Katherine V. Forrest
Cover design by Pat Tong and Bonnie Liss
    (Phoenix Graphics)
Typeset by Sandi Stancil

"Beginning" and "Hope Deferred" were first published in *The Ladder*.
"Sarah Eavesdropping" was first published in the newsletter of New York Daughters of Bilitis.

Library of Congress Cataloging-in-Publication Data

Miller, Isabel, 1924–
    A dooryard full of flowers / by Isabel Miller.
        p.   cm.
    ISBN 1-56280-029-9 : $9.95
    1. Lesbians—Fiction.   I. Title.
PS3563.I39D66   1993
813'.54—dc20   92-40090
                                                        CIP

TO MY BAREFOOT DOCTOR ALL OVER,
WITH LOVE AND THANKS

CONTENTS

Stories

Notebook

Poems

A NOTE FROM THE AUTHOR

Barbara Grier of Naiad Press tells me that *Patience and Sarah* ends as though it's seven o'clock and I have a dinner engagement at eight. That's because I meant to tell the story in two books, the first to be called *A Place for Us*, in which the lovers find each other, make their getaway, and establish their home, the second to be called *A Time for Us*, which would show them in their slow, ardent, exalted life together.

I wrote two chapters of the second, and then hit a block I could never recover from. They moldered in my file until it occurred to me to ask that same Barbara Grier to publish them, pamphlet-size, like a book of poems.

"Can't," she said. "There's a minimum number of pages that can be perfect-bound."

"Fold it over and staple it?"

"Can't. Booksellers won't touch a book that doesn't have a spine. They have enough trouble with books with titles that show."

"What if I look through my file again and see if there's enough there to bring it up to size?"

"Good."

So "A Dooryard Full of Flowers" is plucked from oblivion and brought to the women who wish they knew more about Patience and Sarah.

Two stories from *The Ladder,* "Hope Deferred" and "Beginning," are also here.

From years of notebooks, I chose only "The Night the Curse Was Blessed." When the rest of the record in those notebooks has become merely history, merely the tiny and far-off doings of New York City dykes at the beginning of our revolution, maybe it can be published too.

My file was not the treasure I might have imagined if it had been lost — it was mostly awkward beginnings — but I did find a few stories that seemed worth fixing. In reworking and finishing them, and writing some new ones, I became fond of short stories. They don't ask for years of concentration as a novel does, and they gather up scraps of memory and imagination that have no other places. They let me almost dare to imagine getting my whole life harvested and safe in the barn.

A DOORYARD FULL OF FLOWERS
Portrait by a Neighbor: Klaus

A pair of old maids from back East went and bought that place of More's up on the road to Greenville. They've had a brand-new cedar-shingle roof put onto that worthless old leftover falling-down log cabin, and they've settled in like to stay. Myself, I haven't been asked inside yet, nor any man, but my wife has and she says they've fixed it up pleasant. All they've got for furniture, she says, is a homemade bedstead, but it's got a first-rate quilt on it, she says, and they've put up shelves with fancy dishes lined up along, and they've put up curtains

1

and pictures. You don't even miss proper things much, my wife says. Now *she* wants pictures. Twenty-eight years we've lived without them, but try and tell her that.

These two females say they hope to maintain themselves by farming. Why pick eastern York State, now the West is safe and the Canal's going through, if you want to farm? But I do believe that's their intent. Any other fool can see, they'll live up what money they brought along and then go back to where they came from. Wherever that is. They don't say. "East," they say, and when you say, "Whereabouts in the East?" they look sad and look away, so you feel you're on touchy ground, and make up your mind to let some more blundery person peck it out of them and tell you later.

They must go back, unless they marry. At first sight of them, several rash young fools got marrying thoughts, taken in by prettiness and spirit and never stopping to ask what's the good of a wife that thinks she knows as much as you? I wouldn't marry either of them. I mean, not even if I could.

My own two boys managed to rise above their natural backwardness and start laying claim. They've been up to the ladies' place a lot already, helping them get started. The more help the ladies get the longer they'll last at farming and the later they'll marry, but I don't mention that to my boys. I see no hurry to get the ladies married. I'd like to see them stay like they are, for a while, independent.

I admire their independence. I never said I didn't. I only said I wouldn't marry it, myself. I tell my boys so. As well talk to the wind. Except they turn an unhealthy red, I'd think they didn't hear at

2

all. Sometimes they snicker foolish too, but off they go up the road, just more than praying the ladies'll have some big heavy job to do, something that takes a broad back and not much brain.

The flaw in a fine biddable wife like mine is, she gives you sons that are muscle all the way to their hat. My daughters, they favored me, but what was the good of that? Sometimes I almost wish, now I see it can maybe happen, that my girls was off fending for themselves somewhere, too, instead of married. But then I remind myself how that peculiar household up on Red Mill Road must come to grief, and in a little while I'm sensible again.

Still, while it lasts, there's a lift in seeing pretty women with happy faces. It does the whole neighborhood good to have them. They smile easy. Even the womenfolk feel the good of it.

We all help out, what we can. In pity at their late start — they didn't get settled in till the end of May — some of us spared them some spring chicks cheap. It may be there'll end up more cocks than pullets, but the price was right and the thought is what counts and nothing commands a Christian to be a simpleton.

It's a busy season so we can't pitch in and raise them a barn or like that. Wouldn't that be foolish anyway, being as they can't last a year? And they've got a little log shed that'll be all they're apt to need. Even my boys can't help out as much as they'd like to. I see to that.

But we all, now and again, make gifts, like a loaf of new-baked bread or a dressed hen or a mess of greens or some eggs or a handful of garden seeds or half-a-dozen hop vine sets. My wife took sweet william sets, and then crawled around the dooryard with Miss Patience planting them, and I never heard her laugh and chatter so much — her with her stove-in knees I've heard so much about! In her own way she's as bad as the boys, ready to do more for Miss Patience than for her own.

Miss Patience is the older one. Miss Patience White. She's crowding thirty, by my guess, but my son Ep's sure she's no more than twenty-three. That's because he's twenty-three. She's the one that makes the pictures and does the little female homey things. She's got red hair but she's pretty anyway, and she's got soft pretty little ways about her. After while you don't mind the red hair. You get to think it's not so very red after all. You get to think it's on the brown side. The flaw in her is, she won't be told. She don't argue, not out loud, but no matter what you say, you can see she holds her own opinion in spite of you. That's her only flaw. Aside from that, she just wants you to be comfortable, even when all she can offer as a seat is an overturned bucket amongst the flowers in the dooryard, and she keeps her eye on your cup so it don't run dry.

Miss Patience will be just exactly no good at all at farming. It'll be up to the other one. Her name's Miss Sarah Dowling.

She's the one my son Nate is praying for. He first got a look at her when he was helping the carpenter put that foolish new roof on, and he looked out above the rise and saw her planting her corn. He couldn't get over how neat and easy she did it. He couldn't get over anything about her.

I admit she's a fine tall one, plenty of muscle

and go. Folks say she's handy as a man with hammer or ax or gun. It was talked of everywhere, how she collected the wolf bounty the first week she was here. She can do the lighter men's jobs if she eases into them. Some claim they've seen her wear men's clothes as well, out in her fields, but I haven't seen that myself. Nate says it's not so, but he wouldn't speak against her so I don't put much weight on his testimony. In town she looks like any other woman, only a little stridier.

And she did wear skirts and even a bonnet the day her and me set out the berry bushes I took her. Wouldn't that have been the time to wear britches if she was in the habit of it? And yet I keep hearing she does. In some ways I hope she does. In some ways it would be a sight to see.

Miss Sarah didn't want any help at all with planting the berries, but Nate and me tagged on out despite her. She was bound she'd dig the holes herself, and I was curious how she'd find a place for holes amongst the rocks so I let her. Naturally she didn't want to waste unrocky ground on berries. I just stood there studying her and enjoying myself till time for me to cover the roots. She let me do that much. Nate, big ox, was fetching water to puddle them in with, proud as if it was milk for Cleopatrie's bath.

I admit, Miss Sarah conducted her spade creditable. If any woman can farm, it's her. But I don't think so. Not in Greene County, anyway, all slatey hills. Even men just barely make a go of it here. If I didn't have my cabinetmaking too, I sure wouldn't be fixed as comfortable as I am.

The truth is, when the hemlocks are gone and

5

the tanneries close down, this whole county will go back to wilderness. Ask anybody, what hemlock soil is good for besides hemlock.

But More pastured on the ladies' land for years, and that helped. They can make a crop or two from what the cattle dropped, and then marry and let menfolk do the worrying, and live at ease like other women.

Our preacher's a busy man, with a livery stable to make his living at, so he's not out jawboning his flock much or doing much to increase it. But Ep and Nate kept at him till he did go see Miss Patience and Miss Sarah and get them to say they'd attend our meeting. Better us than the Methodists or the Episcopals, we all figured, and anyway we're handiest.

The ladies set the preacher on that overturned bucket outside and listened to how he came to know what God required of him. We've all heard many times how he found his little daughter trying to put her hand into boiling water, to harden herself for hell, and how he set at praying and Bible-reading to see if God could want either boiling water or hell for a little girl, and how, simple stablekeeper though he be, he ended up figuring he knew more than lots of his betters, and I admit I figure he does too. Which don't mean I never miss a meeting, but when I do go, it's there.

Our church has a lot to be said for it. The preacher gets no pay. We have no building and we're not collecting to get one. Sundays we rent the schoolhouse in Freehold. It works out. Our preacher's a decent man who does no harm. Name me another you can say the same of.

I haven't missed a Sunday since Miss Patience and Miss Sarah agreed to come. Male attendance in general has been remarkable. It always looks like Miss Patience and Miss Sarah won't come, but at the last minute they usually do. There's never any seats left by then except up front, so we all get a good look at them. Miss Patience is still looking sleepy. Miss Sarah is wide awake but not enthusiastic. I believe Miss Patience don't like mornings and Miss Sarah don't like church, but I keep that to myself lest somebody hold it against them.

The singing wakes Miss Patience up. She knows all the words to all the verses of everything, and sings out good except she keeps looking like she wants to laugh. Maybe it's Miss Sarah moving her jaw up and down but not letting out a sound that she's laughing at. Or maybe she's accustomed to a fancy church with musical instruments instead of the likes of us, dragging along one jump behind the loudest voice and more or less making the tune up as we go along. I do suspect her of a fancy church, and I suspect Miss Sarah of no church at all.

Right away my boys decided Miss Patience and Miss Sarah had to take Sunday dinner with us. I knew my wife would like that better than most anything, but the boys didn't know it and they set themselves to bring her round. She held out for a couple of weeks, and got the most chores for the least nagging of all time, and then rather than let them lose heart she said, "All right, all right, I'll ask them after meeting, but it won't look right." To make it look right, I concluded to ask the preacher and his family too.

Then the scouring and scrubbing and polishing and setting out to air, all without my wife having to so much as suggest it. The boys beat the parlor carpet and oiled the floors and washed every window in the house, and they were going to wash the curtains too but my wife wouldn't trust them with that. She did that.

I'd match my house against anybody's, and I figured my boys knew how good it is. I certainly spent enough years telling them how lucky they were. I figured they wanted to show the ladies that we're a well-off family and live in a good plain solid house. And maybe that was the first idea. But as the boys cleaned along, taking what was maybe their first good close look, they got to fretting over every little thing that was faded or scratched or torn or shabby or broken until I was out of patience with them and would hear no more. Except I wanted the young ladies to dinner too, I would have ended the project. All that's the matter with my house is that big clumsy ruffianly boys grew up in it and growing up hasn't improved them. It's maybe made them worse, because now I can't smack them.

But thinking about them growing up, past all the birthdays the others didn't get beyond, and past all the marks in the doorframe the others didn't get taller than, makes me willing to put up with them. It reminds me of the nights I used to get out of bed to make sure Ep and Nate and their sisters were breathing, and find my wife already there leaning over them in the dark and listening too. It reminds me of what their breathing meant, and would mean again. And means right now.

Well, Sunday came and the house was ready and the horses brushed and the buggy washed. A good big dinner was buried in the kitchen coals, and off we went.

After meeting, my wife didn't lose a minute. The fear was — and I felt it too, even if I did keep up a smirk as was my duty — the fear was that somebody else would get to Miss Patience and Miss Sarah first with an invite. Several young men, like didn't come to meeting once in five years ordinarily, were nudging their mothers and sisters to get them to go be friendly, but planning ahead paid off as usual and my wife came back with a lady on each arm, and I could see, knowing her like I do, she was as proud as if she was a young sport herself.

We had to stand around socializing until the preacher locked up and gathered in his wife and youngsters, for what was the good of asking his whole hungry crew unless folks could bear witness that we weren't taking two marriageable females home alone with two marriageable males? The whole time my wife kept a grip on her prizes.

I can read my wife like a book, and I could plainly see she was planning the double wedding and then what three women could do to my place along the line of pictures and flowers and pretties, things one woman alone has a hard time holding out for against three sensible men. She was feeling her voting power tripled. She forgot that three naughts are still naught. She maybe never knew it.

* * * * *

I expect the most interesting event that whole Sunday was when Miss Sarah took her bonnet off. She kept it on as long as she could, saying she didn't want to go inside on such a fine day and couldn't she just walk out and see my crops and the barn and the livestock and all? It was an uncommon thing for a woman to want, but I just laid it to her being an uncommon woman and thought no more about it. I was ready to start right off with her, but Miss Patience gave Miss Sarah a quick little scowl and shook her head a mite, and Miss Sarah sighed and came on inside. It was for all the world like you see husbands and wives do. Then my wife started saying, like women do, "Lay off your wraps now, be comfortable now," and Miss Patience gave Miss Sarah a little nod. At first Miss Sarah looked worried, but then she shrugged her shoulders and laid her bonnet off.

And there she stood with about as much hair on her as the preacher, just enough of it to make a tail tied up behind and not what you'd call a long tail at that.

My wife blurts out, "Why, where's your hair?"

"It went," Miss Sarah says.

My wife says, "Well, I *see* that. *How'd* it go? By itself?"

Miss Sarah says, "Well," and she's looking worried again and I think she just has no idea at all what to say next.

And then the preacher's wife says, "Was it a fever?"

Miss Sarah looks at Miss Patience to find out what to say, and Miss Patience says, "Yes, you could call it that. A fever. A very high fever. Took her hair away." And then Miss Patience sort of whispered behind her hand, but loud enough the whole room of us could hear, "She doesn't like it noticed."

Then I got busy telling the preacher what a fine sermon he preached, and the preacher's wife started swatting her youngsters to keep them from snooping over the house, and my wife took the lids off the pots and gave the dinner a sniff but my big stupid boys just stood there staring at poor Miss Sarah until I took and shoved them out the door. I was plain mortified at them. I would've sold the pair of them for a cent.

My wife stayed down sniffing at the dinner longer than there was any call for, until I finally saw she was sniffing that other way she has that means she's peevy. That's best ignored, and in time it goes away. I don't encourage it by making much of it. There's nothing to do for it anyway. Best thing to do is walk away.

I just took the preacher by the arm and we went outside. The boys were out by the barn sulking. I had a little fatherly talk with them about being such big lummoxes no female in her right mind would look at them.

The preacher said, "Yes, it does seem like boys nowadays are awkwarder and backwarder than in my day."

It's times like that you find out you love your boys. *I'm* the only one that can say such things. If it hadn't been the Sabbath and him the preacher, I'd've knocked him down.

Instead, I merely said, "Any female that don't value steady manly worth should be cursed by having to marry a preacher." That contented me and perked the boys up. I don't know what it did to the preacher.

Everything looked smoothened down amongst the womenfolk when we went inside to ask wasn't it time to eat and groan at them to hurry. Women like us to do that, though they claim not. All but Miss Sarah were getting the food laid out, the last-minute things like biscuits.

Miss Sarah had the preacher's youngsters gathered around her and she was telling them about ships and seagulls and a big whirlpool in a place called Hell's Gate down by New-York full of sucked-down treasures nobody can ever get at. It was the orderliest I ever saw those children. They just fell in love with Miss Sarah. She told them about lands where they eat their salad unboiled, and lands where they won't kill so much as a flea, and lands where it's never winter and others where it's never summer, and lands where grown women have feet no more than two inches long. Some of that I didn't necessarily believe, but I got so interested I almost felt in no hurry for my dinner.

Then afterwards the women did up the dishes out on the bench under the apple tree because the kitchen was a mite hot, and they sang hymns till they loosened the little green apples, I wouldn't doubt. It made kind of pleasant listening except you had to wonder why womenfolk should get all the enjoyment while men just had to sit around in showing-out clothes and be solemn. It wasn't natural for the boys, but I kept them down. If they're old enough to marry, they're old enough to stay still a while.

When the dishes were all polished and put away, my wife took the ladies to the parlor and brought out all the things she always shows — same as I always show my livestock. She showed some dried-up brown flowers from our daughters' weddings, and the little gowns and knitted bootlets the boys got christened in, and the various fancy stitching and prettyfying she goes in for — women things. She did kind of hog Miss Patience and Miss Sarah. I thought she might've let the boys get a little better acquainted, or anyway she might've put in a few words in their behalf, but on the other hand I was glad to see her acting pleasant. I was foolish enough, even after all these years of experience, to believe she wasn't peevish anymore.

So it was quite an upset that night when her and me were alone and I was saying how the day went pretty good, all things considered, to have her sniff peevish again and say she wouldn't have the ladies back because, she said, "They're fancy and peculiar."

It shows the falseness of the female that she treated them so pleasant face to face.

What she couldn't forgive was being made to feel in the wrong for noticing Miss Sarah's hair, what there was of it, and speaking of it. " 'She don't like it noticed,' " my wife says, high and mean, which wasn't a good imitation of Miss Patience at all. My wife says, "Like it's me to be shamed for seeing it, stead of her for having it!"

You just never know what's going to hurt a woman's feelings. It's no use trying to know.

I made the mistake, for a while, of trying to say our new friends have a good side too, but I only made it worse so I stopped. Least said, soonest mended. She'll come round. She'll have to. For I've decided to let Ep and Nate go through with the marrying. Foolish though I be, I'd put up with a lot of grief to get that singing and laughing and storytelling into my house every day.

It was while I was laying there in the dark fixing the day's events in my mind, that I begun to see a few things about Miss Patience and Miss Sarah. Begun to see their secret.

Folks say it's the sadness of their past that keeps the ladies from speaking of it. Broken hearts, lovers killed in war, nonsense ideas like that folks have. I marvel they can't see the laugh in the ladies' eyes when they bend their heads and try to look upset enough so you won't have the heart to pry.

No, it's not sadness they're hiding — but I'm ready to let everybody go on thinking so. I'll never tell it around, what I came to see on that night of remembering.

What is that *air* they have, I asked myself — where have I seen that before? I was so misled by their poor little house and their stony farm that I couldn't see for a while that their air is *money*. Once I saw it, I was mortified it took me so long. The whole way they walk and talk and wear their plain unshowy clothes should've told me, their whole way of being pleased about help but not really needing it, the way they're unbeholden, the way they're not humble. What but money can make heads stand up like theirs do?

So it's money they're keeping still about when they won't speak of the past. Well, at first I thought that was modest and pleasant enough, unbraggy, but

I kept on thinking and it began to seem unnatural. Most moneyed folk will let the fact be dragged from them fast enough. Even when it's evil money — pirate money, slave money, smuggling money — whatever it is, they figure out a way to put a good face on it. And most moneyed women don't leave the protection of their family and buy the worst house they can find and start to play at farming. So was there money once but no more? Well, I didn't think so. Losing money hits folks terrible hard, harder than losing reputation even, and it's plain that Miss Patience and Miss Sarah haven't been hit by anything. That is, not anything hard to bear.

So there I was, stumped, but I've found that thoughts will sort themselves out if you turn your back on them a while, and I went on remembering the day, and how Miss Sarah looked with the preacher's youngsters crowded around her, and how her face was so affectionate and full of laugh and self-forgetting and lively and pretty, and her hair skun back smooth and tied just almost like a man's. How she looked, what it added up to, she looked like just about the handsomest *boy* in the world.

Thanks to the careful looking-over I gave her the day we set out the berries, I wasted no time wondering *is* Miss Sarah, after all, a boy. She's a female all right, no question. A fine one, with good hips for bearing. She can give me my grandsons without whining and not be worthless after just nine or ten neither. Miss Patience I can't count on the same way. She'll know too many female ways to take advantage, and I admit bearing might not be as easy for her. There might be cause. I doubt her hips have got the breadth of bone in them, for all they

15

look like such a good handful when the wind blows right to plaster her skirts up against her.

I laid there, happy, thinking how to raise the grandsons and wondering if I should let them be told of faraway lands. On the one hand it would keep their brain stimulated, but on the other hand it would make them harder to keep where they belong. Who could say but what hearing such stories was what made Miss Sarah herself not stay where she belonged?

I could be glad for my own sake that she did what she did, and still feel some pity for whoever let her get ideas and paid the price by having her run off. I tried to picture in my mind who could've done such a foolish thing. I've known my share of fools, but not any as foolish as that, not men, and what woman would know enough?

So I was stumped again, and it wasn't till the next day when I was gluing and clamping a chair, reflecting like you will at a job like that, that it came to me. Nobody told Miss Sarah about those far-off lands, she knows all that her own self! She's been on ships, she's been across the sea! What could she be but a captain's daughter? Many a captain's daughter is born on a long voyage, and what's to keep one now and then from just staying on with her father, and growing up on his ship? Especially if her mother's dead? And it's plain that Miss Sarah has no mother.

The shipboard life explains the money. It explains the short hair — for wouldn't her father want her to seem a boy on a ship full of sailors? It explains why a girl of her quality knows nothing about church. It explains why her father let her go — he couldn't keep her on a ship her whole life long. Or did she run away? Did she hate the ship, and pine for land and farming, like so many that want the contrary to what they have?

I'm satisfied I understand Miss Sarah now, all except how she got a little soft Eastern gentlewoman to come farming with her. Now I have to turn Miss Patience in my mind. In time, I'll understand her too. I'd rather work it out for myself than ask her, considering she won't tell me anyhow.

A Closer View: Sarah

We liked to walk out over our fields of an evening after supper, to keep track of how everything came along and to give George a run, which he could've had by himself any time, but he didn't want to without us. I knew how he felt from how I felt about Patience, so I didn't try to change him, even though it might've been better if he'd stayed back and watched over the house.

All day those first days, I'd find a job that would keep me by her, like patching at the cattle shed or building a bench for the washtub or pounding together a chicken coop. It was all needed, but it ran so easy because it kept me near Patience, as to make me worry the whole time that I was shirking. I worried I should be in the fields instead.

And every evening when we walked out, I'd see the time come closer when I must be at our crops, away from Patience. The oats and hay came along all right by themselves, and the corn was too small to bear a hoeing. But the taters — they weighed on me.

George would be trotting ahead with his tail in a big easy fluffy curl, and Patience would be saying, "See how the new chinking makes our house look white from here. See how the sunset lights our windows gold." I'd just be seeing the weeds and the crust on the soil, feeling bad but saying nothing. Then the tater bugs showed up, and they settled it.

We walked back to the house. It was getting to look like a home. I just loved the look of that true ridgeline. The hop vines were starting up the walls on either side of the door. There was dark enough to show the first brightest stars and the fireflies, and to hide us, so I took her by the hand and said, "There's no more putting it off. I got to work the taters tomorrow."

"You say it like a last farewell," Patience said.

"I don't want to leave you."

"Leave me? I'll be with you."

I said, "Oh, no," and "It's not fitten," and like that, but next morning when I put the hoe over my shoulder and started out, she was by me.

It was a real fine June day.

She said, "We wouldn't want it said we parcel the work out like imitation man and wife, you in the fields, I in the house."

"Why wouldn't we want it said, if it's how it is?"

"There's plenty that is, that we wouldn't want said."

I could see some truth in that, but nothing made me admit it. I just asked her, "Are you back at fretting over what might be said?"

She said, "Well, there's a difference between being found out when we still have the West to run to, and being found out when we're already in the West and have put all our money into it." I was grateful she'd call Greene County, New York, West. She had her ups and downs on that. Some days she'd say it wasn't enough like her dream. "Beware," she'd say in her schoolmarmy way, with her finger up, "beware of taking away a woman's dream." To me it seemed better than the dream, not to be like my Pa trying to farm between girdled trees and stumps, but if it would make her feel like a real pioneer in the real West, to be working a tater field we'd bought ready-planted in eastern York State, it seemed best not to tell her better.

She said, "We'll spell each other," which meant I was to pull off bugs while she hoed up one row and back the next, and then the other way round. It was nonsense, being as we only had one hoe, and I couldn't believe a soft lady like her would want to pull many bugs. One or two bugs would do her, I figured. And spelling each other was a waste of time. It's best to get into the swing of a job and stay with it.

She'd never hoed in her life, and she didn't have the clothes for it. There she was in the shoes she'd kept school in, and a long wide skirt that got in her way every move she made, and tight sleeves. She chopped straight up and down instead of slanting to cut the roots of the weeds, and she hit too close for comfort to the tater bushes. I could just barely keep my mind on my own job for worrying about hers.

I let her do half her stint, and then I ran down

and caught ahold of the hoe. She hung on pretty good, for a little woman, but then I kissed her knuckles and she let go.

She said, "I could do it, if I had britches like you."

But in just that little time, her face was moist already and the little strands I like so much along her back hairline were curled up tight, little foxy o's.

I said, "No you couldn't, honey. And I've made my mind up not to let you."

I sure had a lot to learn. I say in excuse we'd only been together full time for — March, April, May — three months and part of June. She raised her eyebrows and said, very ladylike, "I shall have britches, and I shall win the hoeing competition at the Agricultural Fair."

There was nothing for it but I must go back to the house with her and get out of my britches so she could have them as a guide to make her own. Without them I couldn't go back outside, and for a while it seemed like I could just hear the little sharp teeth of the tater bugs chomping away. I got on the bed frontside down and put my chin in my hands and pouted at her, but then the sight of her sort of won me over and I decided that what there was no help for I might as well enjoy.

First she put my britches on herself, blue broad-falls, not overclean, and too long for her, and baggy on her. I wanted to laugh, how out of place they looked with her white chemise with the silken ribbon threaded through the top. But she wasn't thinking about maybe being comical. She was thinking what to allow for our difference in size. She was working. I do love the look on her face when she's thinking and working. I stayed real quiet, not to spoil it.

Then she opened one of the trunks, and the good smell of herbs came at me. I love it when the trunks get opened. It made me feel so snuggish, so sort of prepared for anything, to have her take out shears and thread, and a packet of needles and pins, and newspapers, and lengths of cloth to choose among, indigo and madder and walnut she'd dyed herself back home, and some store-boughten goods I couldn't figure out what they got the colors from. She picked out a sensible one, walnut, already dirt-colored. It always catches me unready, to have her do something sensible like that. I almost thought for a minute she maybe knew what field work meant — her that never liked to sweat or get her hands dirty! I even let myself fancy how sweet it would be, to have her by me in the fields, and how pretty her soft round jiggly hindermost would look in walnut that fit a little near. I want to say I never did suppose it would make the neighbors take less of an interest in us.

Patience set right at pinning the newspapers together, and flapping the britches this way and that, pinning up long tucks in them, all very fast and neat, all the while explaining this is how you make a paper pattern and how you make it fit you and it was as pretty to me, hearing her, as the song of a bird, and I made just about as much sense out of it.

Then just out of nowhere, she looked at me sharp and asked, "Are you paying attention?"

It pulled me up, like awake from a happy dream. Well, of *course* I was paying attention. I could've made a picture of how she looked in her drawers and chemise and knotted-top blue stockings, squatting on the floor and snipping the newspaper into curves and straights. The bright shears. Her freckly hands and white arms. I didn't figure I'd missed much of importance.

"Well, naturally," I said, trying for her same touch of sharpness to end the subject, but she just held out the shears to me and said, "In that case, you cut the pattern for the back half, now that you know how."

"No I don't either know how," I said, but I did go stand by her. There's no real good way not to do what she's made up her mind for me to.

"I'm teaching you," she said.

"I don't want to know how," I said.

"But that's the plan. I'll plant and hoe and mow with you, and you'll sew and cook and clean with me."

"Who gets up these plans? *I* never had that plan."

"Come on, Sarah honey."

She is a woman of terrible firm ideas. I had the name for that myself at one time, but I was never in the same class of it as Patience.

So there I was on my knees trying to make my britches stay flat so I could pin them down and cut around them, and talking barn talk and making a few little mistakes apurpose to get her to say, like I'd said about the hoe, "You're hopeless. Here, give me that."

But she just stayed as easy as you please, on the bed where I'd been, with her chin in her hands and a peaceful expression, like she didn't have a doubt about me, and I could see she meant to hold me to it.

I said it seemed to me we ought to each do what we knew best and not just hack and blunder away doing hard what the other could do as easy and pretty as play. (All the while I was cutting a more-or-less pattern piece, kind of raggedy because my britches was a little bulged-out behind so if I pushed them down one place they'd pop up another, and I never could say for sure just where any one edge really came.)

Patience said, "You can fret all you please, but I'm going to be sure you know all the womanly arts so you can keep yourself fed and clothed and cozy, and keep me too after I get too old to manage."

Six years seemed to her like such a big gap between us, like I'd be spry when she was doddering. To me, just six years never mattered much, except I expect it was one reason I let her boss me more than I ever felt I could boss her back. Another reason I let her was that she was an educated woman, and I'd only just learned to read the summer before, when I was already twenty-two. And another reason was, it was her inheritance money that got us out of Connecticut and off here with our own place, and even though I knew she didn't the least bit begrudge me, I figured I'd feel better once I'd made a crop and sold it.

So all those reasons, and some others, kept me at that foolishness with the pattern, and then she said, "Watch how I cut the cloth," but I snuck back into my britches and hurried back to the taters.

It just gave George a fit to have us two places and him only one dog, but then he settled on me.

He was always my dog at heart. I don't think Patience ever really felt for him, though she was agreeable to everything I showed her about him. I showed her it was wonderful how somebody that wasn't even a person could *look* at you. I never could say right what I meant. I can't now either. I'd say, "You'd sure think it was wonderful if a *tree* looked at you," and she'd say, "Yes, indeed I would," in the blandest way, not thinking.

I couldn't make her think about George. I'd show her how we should admire the ways he was better than us, and pity the ways he was worse, and be thankful he chose us to live with, and she'd just agree and agree. I wanted her to fight a while, and then have it hit her how right I was, and *then* agree. It was all what my friend Parson Peel had showed me, only he'd used his horse Potiphar as an example instead of a dog. I had to wonder if I was quicker than Patience, or if Parson was better than me at showing, or if a horse is just naturally more mysterious than a dog.

I got in about three good solid hours with the taters, and then I begun to want my dinner and the sun was at the peak of the sky so I figured I was entitled and I stuck the hoe handle into the ground and lit off for the house, George too.

Patience was sitting under the apple tree in the yard, on the turned-over bucket. She had her lap full of that walnut-colored cloth and she was stitching away, which would've been a pretty sight ordinarily but I have to admit it hurt me right then, me so hungry and her knowing I must be, and caring no more than that.

I stopped a ways back from her, to get myself in

hand before she could see, and I run it over in my mind, how she wasn't my servant nor my slave, and if she'd wanted no more from life than to cook dinner day-in day-out for a farmer she'd've married a man instead of me, and hadn't she said I was to cook and sew and clean along with her? So I straightened myself out and stopped feeling hurt. I made my mind up to say nothing, and just cook our dinner myself as best I could, even if it meant I couldn't get back to the field the rest of the day.

I walked past her without saying anything, for fear my fool voice would show something. The door was open and when I got near it I started to smell something. I sort of thought, and then I knew, it was a fine stew bubbling over the fire and I thought how lucky it was I'd held my tongue, and then on the trunk, which was what we still used for a table at that time, I saw a cake.

Patience came up behind me and put her arms around me and I turned around and bent my head down to her shoulder and cried, because it didn't seem fair that I should have everything so fine and beautiful and the rest of the people in the world not.

HOPE DEFERRED

When I was in the Navy, I had a bunkmate named Patty. What I liked best about her at first was that I didn't like her very much, and I thought I could experience, at last, an ordinary girl-girl friendship without any wear and tear. It was too tiresome, loving, and choking on my heart, and maintaining throughout a pleasant expression, more or less. Patty was a very ordinary girl, only approximately pretty, not amusing, not understanding, cold. Her mind, though possibly good, was given nothing to grow on. She didn't read anything or listen to anything. All told, she was exactly what I needed. How it rejoiced me to feel nothing when we walked together. It went on that way for weeks, no hopes, no longings, just peace.

The first warning that peace was too good to last came one morning when we were late for breakfast and she had a catch in her side and couldn't run. I started to hurry ahead without her. Then I looked back and saw her struggling along like an old woman, and I felt the frightening beginning of tenderness for her. I didn't let it take hold, though. I waited impatiently, like a normal girl, and complained like a normal girl, and I fooled even myself that I was going to be able to get out of loving her.

We went out together every weekend, to drink-dance places and picked up, or let ourselves be picked up by, sailors. She kissed hers, I kissed mine, all very dull and calm.

Then one night the sailors were different — they had a place to go (an almost-abandoned Navy dispensary) and an ambulance, also Navy, to get there in. Protected by youth, stupidity, and complete heterosexual anesthesia, I wasn't afraid to go. Patty's reasons may have been about the same.

World War II was over. These sailors were the final skeleton crew of their little hospital. One sailor was short and dark and the other tall and blond. There was nobody else for miles around. They gave us drinks made of grapefruit juice and medical alcohol. There wasn't enough alcohol for the second round so they had to make-do with elixir-terpin-hydrate with codeine, a cough medicine. It was unspeakable so I wouldn't drink mine, but Patty drank hers. Maybe more than one. I didn't know, because I allowed myself to be lured off to an empty ward by the tall blond sailor.

He was a nice boy, not much more interested in me than I was in him. His attempt was mild, standard, easily rebuffed, and not renewed. We talked about books and movies, and when we figured we'd stayed away our decent interval we went back to our buddies.

Patty was in the bathroom, vomiting. She had all her clothes on except her jacket. I thought she'd had no more trouble with her sailor than I with mine.

They took us to our barracks in the ambulance. There was a larky young feeling about going home that way, except that Patty wasn't looking larky. As she was getting out her sailor said, "Now what was your name again?" and to my surprise, instead of laughing or lying, she told him, first name and last, accurate in every part.

So then I knew.

Going up the stairs she told me. She was so sick and scared. She smelled awful, from the vomit and the other. Puffy and blotchy with tears. So I loved her.

"Okay, I won't tell anybody, and don't you either," I said.

She wanted to go straight to bed but I wouldn't let her. "Looking like this tomorrow is telling everybody about tonight," I said and bossed her to the shower. She bathed herself. I didn't dare help her, and anyway she didn't need help. Afterwards I put her hair up in pincurls, wrapped her net around her head, and boosted her into her upper bunk. Then I lay awake for hours, scared because I loved her.

Next day she was clearer-headed, and therefore on the verge of nervous collapse. There wasn't a hope, she said, that she wasn't pregnant. She didn't know what to do. I didn't know either, but providence came along and showed me.

Patty and I were sitting in the lounge, I trying to hide my love and at the same time to spread it over her to protect her, and she just looking grim and starey like somebody wandering away from a bomb blast, when one of the new Waves came in and said, "Anybody want a blind date for tonight?" Nobody ever did and only a new girl would ask. "They're real cute," she said. "One's tall and blond and the other's short and dark."

"I do," I said.

"Which one?"

"Short and dark."

I was right on the spot when he pulled up in his ambulance.

"You," he said.

"Ummhmm."

"Where's Patty?"

"Upstairs."

"I'd like to see her."

That was gentlemanly, and since he was a well-built young man and seemed intelligent, I saw that one solution was to get him to marry her. I went up to get her. At first she said she wouldn't see him, but then she said she would, so I put a clean shirt on her and combed her hair. "Stand proud now," I said.

She said she would, but she didn't. She looked like a whipped hound.

He said, "You okay?"

She said, "I guess so," and scurried back upstairs.

Then off to the show we went in the ambulance, which was a Jeep at heart and too noisy for talk, so he had to wait till we got to the theater lobby to ask, "What is this?"

"It's very Biblical. He went in unto her and she conceived and bare a son and they called his name Enoch."

"She told you."

"Yeah."

"And she's scared she's knocked."

"Sure. And since you're a medical man and have lots of alcohol and elixir-terpin-hydrate and codeine, why not something for this, too? What's the word? Abortifacient, I think."

"I haven't got any. Anyway, I'm sterile. I had mumps."

"I'll tell her," I said, with real gratitude.

I enjoyed the movie with a clear mind. If Patty wasn't in trouble she resumed her former role and I didn't have to go through all that loving her would involve.

Afterwards, he and I went back to the scene of the crime. His tall blond buddy wasn't there. I sat on the bed and he in a chair near by.

I said I didn't think he should give virgins codeine and then ravage them. I said it nicely, like a sister who had mostly his spiritual well-being at heart. I really did like him. He said she wasn't a virgin. He said she was the worst, most uninteresting, tamest girl he'd ever taken to bed. I said he should marry her. He said he might consider marrying me, but not her. I thanked him, but no thanks. He said he wanted to be a fireman someday, because firemen have so much time to read.

Then, to my astonishment, he came over and put his arms around me, saying, "Why are we wasting all this time talking?"

I guess he thought that her beautiful description had moved me to seek the same for myself. I succeeded in convincing him that my reason for coming was exactly as stated, all without hurting his feelings, and he was in fair spirits when he took me to my barracks even though, thanks to me, his score that year was only three hundred and sixty-four.

A few days later when I went to Patty's office to pick her up after work, he was there. "Congratulate us, we're getting married," he said.

"That's nice," I said.

"Don't act so surprised. You're the one that talked me into it."

I think he might have married her, too, except that he was due for discharge and eager to go home and be a fireman.

In any case, he had brought her some ergot.

So I had to love her after all.

She didn't wait to see if she really needed the ergot. She just took it, in a panic, in more than the dose he'd typed on the label, and I worried all night but it ended well.

I should have been able to untangle myself then, with everything ended well. But I got worse. In fact, no one before her had been so painful, despite her promising beginning. I noticed that her hair was silky and full of light. That her eyelids were tender and dark. Teeth white. Breasts uneven, one high, one low. Helter-skelter black hairs on her legs, sharp as iron filings and so riotous in their growth that she had to shave them every day. She hated them but I was touched.

She had no thoughts for the future, no fears, no plans. I saw that she would always be in trouble and that I would have to devote my life to getting her out. I would have to think up a way to make a living and seek training for it, seriously and single-mindedly, like a man, with no recreational elective courses like literature and bird identification.

I saw that her lips, which at first had seemed only small, were beautifully cut. My longing was for that mouth. I was to both sexes virgin and had modest goals.

Modest but overpowering. After many weeks, I decided to try.

I had no idea what to do, but need promoted invention, sort of.

First I tried pretending that I was having slight nightmares, hoping she would fling herself on me to comfort me. Maybe she didn't even hear me — I kept my little whimpers low, just right for her, three feet above me, to hear. She may have actually been asleep, for all I know. Sleeping was so inconceivable to me that I always assumed she wasn't. I would lie there under her, looking at the sag her sweet bottom made. There was light from the fire-escape door.

Maybe the Navy's not wanting my kind around was for our own sakes; living in that kind of intimacy would probably kill you after a while.

Next I talked of kissing, enthusiastically, until she said I must be a sex fiend. That hurt me and I retreated. Avoided her.

A few days later, she came looking for me. I was ironing in the basement. Alone. "I'm sorry I said that," she said, "but you did talk funny."

"I meant I wanted to kiss *you*," I said.

She drew back.

"Don't be like that," I said. "A person can't tell you *anything*."

"It's like — queer."

"Yes, I'm queer about you."

"Well, I like you, but not like that."

"Okay, okay," I growled, all hurt pride, in full gallop back to my shell. But then I realized that Patty needed time. The necessary thing, I realized, was to endure remaining vulnerable while Patty's imagination worked on her feeling for me and made her ready.

So I laughed no phony roar, and told no tale of man and engagement, and was left with nothing to say or do. I just ironed away, trying to think up something pleasant.

My silence bothered Patty. "Are you mad at me?" she asked.

"No. Oh, no. I love you," I said, and smiled a perfectly real smile.

From then on I sought in all my contacts with her to show her my tenderness and my respect for her refusal, and my ungoatish readiness in case she should change her mind.

In a mere week or so, this wise policy bore fruit. Patty suggested that we get a hotel room together for the weekend. She wanted a tub bath, she said.

She was tired of showers. And to get drunk without being seen, and to sleep late on Sunday. What she wanted, I knew, was to be mine. I made the hotel reservation, very happy.

We bought whiskey and brandy and bath things — oil, salts, capsules — and went to the hotel. The desk clerk hesitated to let us have the room, despite my reservation, when he saw we were Waves, but when we assured him we wouldn't have men up he said, reluctantly, "All right."

I felt so confident, patient, loving, tender, gentle, not in the least in a hurry. We drew a bath and put some of everything into it. How it foamed! The tub was big. "Room for two," Patty said. I climbed in behind her and held her gently between my legs without pressing. I kept my hands off her, out of delicacy, not to rush. Looked at her lovely skin, loved her. Spend my life taking care of her, loving her, touching that lovely skin.

We dried ourselves. Went to bed. I rolled over and laid my face against her throat and kissed her there. "I love you," I said.

"I like you, but I don't love you," she said.

"Yes you do. You love me and I love you." Kissing along her throat towards her ear.

"Stop it," she said.

I didn't believe a word of it. I reached her ear and caught the lobe.

"If you don't stop it, I'm going back to the base."

Shocked at last. "Would you really?"

"Yes, I would."

So I got up and broke the seal on the brandy and had a drink. It tasted awful. I was a modest drinker then. I read the label on the bottle for a while, and then the Gideon Bible for a while. There was a good line in it: "Hope deferred maketh the heart sick."

Patty was lying there with her back to me, utterly covered. I went to bed carefully, not to touch her. Very far from her. A double bed can be as wide as the sky, I found out that night.

Then across all that space came her foot seeking mine. I thought she was torturing me again. I had never reached my foot across a double bed and I didn't know it can mean only, let's make up. I took my foot away. I suppose sooner or later we slept.

We went back to the base the next day. We were out of money, and tried to sell the unopened whisky to a cab driver but he didn't want it, so I smuggled it into the base in my coat sleeve.

I worked very hard at not loving her. I got engaged to an old boyfriend by mail. I told Patty she wasn't as beautiful as Ingrid Bergman and couldn't possibly be a movie star. I took up with other people, safe from loving them because I loved her. I drank a shot of the whiskey every day. There was no trouble about that, so I guess nobody important smelled me. I wouldn't go out picking up sailors anymore, with her or anyone else. I stayed in and read.

Patty got new buddies. One Saturday night she phoned me. She was at a party, she said, and I should come. She and her new buddies had found these terrific sailors and were having this terrific party, too good to miss. She was giggling full tilt. "I'll come," I said.

I dressed. Stood in the rain for the bus. Found the hotel. Bore the knowing looks from the desk, went up. Patty was on the bed, undressed only to her slip, with a small adolescent sailor. Her buddies and their sailors were necking and giggling all around. Stewed, of course, the lot of them. Laughing repeatedly at one repeated joke the adolescent sailor made: "Pretty soon we'll all be pushing up daisies," and the joke part was when he wet his forefinger and pushed upward with it.

I felt very old, sober, dull, serious, stodgy, and forlorn. I had no place there and no intention except to keep Patty from needing more ergot. She consented to get dressed and come with me.

It was late and we were the only women on the bus. I leaned my head against the window and contemplated the fact that I was the only one on the bus Patty would have had any moral hesitation about going to bed with. Fortunately I was young and therefore mostly unborn myself, and I didn't make a sight of myself by weeping. I felt it as a bitterness, not yet unbearable, that adolescent sailors and aspiring firemen and every other lout that came down the pike had a natural right to her while my honorable protecting love was officially a disease.

The adolescent sailor phoned me for weeks, trying for a date. So I must assume I didn't act as prison-matronly and forbidding as I felt. I told him no, I never swiped my friends' dates.

Patty and I got shipped to a new base. We were just about useless to any base we were assigned to, so we got shipped around whenever there was any shipping. Actually this time a great batch of us went, so many the train didn't want to spare the room to accommodate us properly, and some of us had to double up.

The officer assigned Patty and me to share a berth, because we were sitting together, and I could hardly wait. Then there we were, side by side in a lower berth with the curtains closed, a snug little world. I was by the window, she on the edge. Carefully we didn't touch each other. She whispered that the Navy was stingy to jam us up like this. She whispered that she had the curse and her belly hurt. "Put your hands on it, like a hot-water bottle," I said.

"How?" she said, and though it was self-evident I was glad to show her. "Like this," I said, laying one hand on her belly to warm it. "See how warm?"

But she threw my hand off like it was some huge bug. So much for that. I turned my back to her and raised the window shade a crack, and looked out all night, concentrating on not touching her, not letting one cell of my body touch her.

We settled in at our new base. She needed me until she got acquainted with other people, so I broke down and went drinking with her again.

One night we were at an Aloha-type, pseudo-Hawaiian, bamboo-wall place drinking everything on the list, one of each, for the experience, not to be narrow. I got so wrapped up in the drinking and looking at her and trying to explain to her that she led me on and raised my hopes and then dashed them and how cruel that was, that I forgot we were there to pick up men. It was completely amazing to me to feel a big hand on my shoulder and hear a man say, "What are you *talking* about?" I came tumbling down out of our privacy, but I lit on my feet. He was a Navy flyer and he had an identical friend with him.

"About men, what else?" I said, with a big hello smile. Patty was moving over to let the friend sit beside her. My hero slid in by me. I made conversation. He gazed at me with conventional lust. I didn't dare look at Patty for a while, so I gazed back at him. I had to look someplace. Then out of the corner of my eye I saw that Patty was kissing her Navy flyer.

"She's *kissing* him!" I said to mine.

"Of course," he said, and covered my mouth with his. It didn't matter. I wonder if he wanted to, or if he was in love with his friend and trying to hide it.

Fortunately they had no ambulance and no place to take us, so they walked us to our bus stop and that was that. It was very late. Patty's flyer held her against him and lifted her buttocks with his hands and kissed her. I wouldn't kiss mine anymore. I just hung onto the bus stop sign and said I was drunk and where was the lousy bus?

Next morning, she had a mighty hangover. For some reason, I didn't. A premonition of what a heroic drinker I had it in me to become? She vomited and vomited. I'd read somewhere that tomato juice was curative, so I got on the station bus and went to Ship's Service and bought her a papercupful. She drank it and vomited it up.

Later in the day she felt a little better. I was on my bunk eating crackers and she came out of the shower and lay down beside me and asked for some. I fed them to her. I couldn't believe her mouth could still be so beautiful.

"You're getting crumbs on my face," she said.

"It's in the nature of crackers," I said.

"You got them there, you get them off," she said.

39

I brushed at her face with my hand.

"Not that way," she whispered.

It took a few seconds to work out an alternative, too late, because as I leaned to nibble the crumbs off she rolled away.

She was discharged while I still had time left on my hitch. As the time for her to leave approached, I took to weeping steadily and helplessly whenever I had a moment to myself. I could pull right up when anyone was around, and let down like a conditioned dog when the time was right.

The night before Patty was to leave, she asked for her hair curlers back. "But you don't *use* them," I said. "You don't even *like* them."

"They're mine."

"Let me buy them from you."

But she wouldn't. Maybe she was afraid I'd set them in the center of a little shrine. Maybe I would have. To soothe me for the loss of them, she put my hair up with bobbypins. I was too distraught to enjoy the process.

She was to leave while I was at work, at ten in the morning. I worked up a satisfactory lie for my officer, that I had to catch this lot of girls before they left because one of them owed me five dollars. He was so touched that he assigned a car to take me.

Her group left the barracks a few minutes after I got there. She wasn't alone for a second, so I went down to the lounge to wait for her to go by. When she did, I looked at her, but she didn't look back.

I got discharged. I went home to wait for September, the new academic year. While I was waiting around, I got a letter from Patty. It said, "I think I love you, the same way you love me. I think I did all along."

I could say that the reason I didn't rush to Patty's side on receiving her letter was that she was three thousand miles away, or that I recalled her tendency to be provocative and then when I responded run from me. But the fact is that I never once considered going to her. It just didn't occur to me. I wrote her a sad letter, very cautious and noncommittal, because I remembered what happened to the letters poor Stephen wrote in *The Well of Loneliness*. Also I honorably burned Patty's letter so it could never fall into malicious hands.

A CHANGE OF HEART

Here I am, all mercy-scattering like Florence Nightingale, with my baby girl Becky in her basket. I have come to take care of Amelia, my mother-in-law. She's just home from gall bladder surgery, too soon, to save money. I am glowing with conceit and good intentions. What good is a husband to a sick woman, especially a bitter old grump like Gus? I will tend Amelia in a womanly way, and make sure her clean-scrubbed house stays clean-scrubbed. She will lie on her couch reading her Bible and getting well. It's true she and I don't get along. We are opposites. But I don't even wonder if she wants me here. I am family, and this is what families *do*.

Amelia is a plain, hardworking, dutiful, pious farm wife. I smoke, wear slacks, sleep late, blaspheme, read all the time, and tend to let things slide and then catch up in one heroic burst. But in the two years since I stole Fred, her only child, her favorite person on earth, she has never preached or criticized. She has tried to improve me entirely by example. She also tries to demonstrate that Christians are kind and decent, because I think they're not. I think the thought of me in hell gives them a delicious tingle.

She has worked hard on Christian forbearance. She can start out meaning to reinforce whatever in me gives grounds for hope ("Your simple meals are *nourishing*") and then sincerity intrudes. Without intending to, she's adding something like, "I don't care *what* Gus's brothers say! Fred is *not* getting thin! His eyes are *not* glassy!" Then when I laugh she does too, but she's embarrassed, never having meant to reveal that all of Fred's relatives are distraught, afraid he's getting tuberculosis in my care. I don't mind bitchery, very much. Well, I'm not wild about it, but it's better than saintliness. When Amelia's bitchy, we can both laugh. When she's saintly, neither of us can think of anything except my moral inferiority, which she doesn't know the half of.

She doesn't know — does she even know there can be such a person? — that I am a lesbian trying to remake myself with the love of a good man and a good baby. So far, so good. But I have to be careful. I am a little detached. Aloof. In this world of ordinary people, I feel I have to be. I have to stop loving the ones who without exception don't want me, the women. I have bent too many times on that line. One more bend would snap me. Fred wants me. What a welcome change.

I worry about Becky's having to go through all this. If only she were a boy! She still treats me like the earth, like air, not grateful. She falls asleep against my breast with absolute unreflecting confidence, not a tight muscle anywhere in that dear soft solid tiny body. If she were a boy, she could sleep with a woman every night for a lifetime.

When I study her ears, her curved cheek, her wrinkly knuckles, and watch the slow drift of the ancestors across her face, remembering how their lives went, I think no, no, I cannot bear that the wind should blow upon thee.

While I was pregnant, I visited my parents. My little niece was there too. It fell to me to put her to bed. Lula. She was four. I read her a story, sang her a song, tucked the covers around her, and patted her.

"Lie down with me?" Lula said.

"No. No indeed," I said.

"My mother does."

"Well, I don't," I said, and turned off the light.

I stayed awake a long time grieving for little Lula, my brother's beautiful daughter, and all the useless longing she would have to go through because her mother hadn't distanced her, had let a thing like that get started.

Then I heard my father shouting, "What are you doing in here? Don't you *ever* come in here again!" Lula was crying, but I didn't go to her, didn't say what's the matter, honey, did something scare you, there there everything's okay.

Instead I remembered a night when I was four, like Lula. I spent it wailing to sleep with my mother and being beaten by my father. My sweet tired gentle mother didn't get home much when I was four. She was a nurse. She had to live at the hospital. During the Great Depression, hospitals could get away with that. I missed her with my whole body. When she came home I howled to be held by her. My brother kept saying, "Shut up, here he comes again!" and I kept yelling, "I don't care, I want to sleep with Mama!" I felt that she was longing for me too. I had to fight that huge man for both our sakes. Not to would betray her.

But I had to give up. I felt his strength and my weakness convincingly. Neither of us ever forgot.

"I had to spank your brother just once," he'd say every year or so. "And I had to spank *you* once, and you never did get over it."

"No, I never did," I'd say.

"I had to do it," he'd say.

"Yeah," I'd say, sullenly, until I was older than he was the night he spanked me.

The happy ending will come. In his old age, he will admit, "Course Mama wouldn't speak to me all night." (He was big and butchy, but never too proud to call my mother Mama.)

So I won after all. I wish I'd known it sooner.

Then another ending, maybe the last one. My

brother will tell me our dad wept on his deathbed, wishing he could have figured out how to talk to me. I will almost disbelieve. I have felt so certain of his dislike. But my brother could never lie about something so important and solemn. My dad loved me. I wish I'd known it sooner.

No, one more ending. I will dream I'm at a party with my dad, on a solid concrete pier, and he takes a step backward and falls into the water. He can't swim and neither can I, and even if we could there's nothing on the pier to pull ourselves up by. It's a solid block. But I have to try. I lie on the pier and stretch my hand down to him. He's reaching up. I can barely touch his hand. I think he's too big, too heavy, there's nothing I can do, but I have to try. I clasp his hand and pull, and he flies up out of the water like a fish and lands on his feet on the pier. Then he's sitting with some other people at a table. I wonder if he's cold from the water. I go over and put my hand on his neck inside his collar. He is warm and dry.

We are healed at last, even though it's too late to talk.

But I didn't yet know any of these endings on the night he drove Lula back to her lonely scary bed and I was his silent accomplice. Was I still afraid of him, even though I had resisted him about everything for years? Did I want Lula to fail as I had — not sleep with my mama, not do what I had broken my heart to do but still not done? No, by then I reluctantly agreed with my dad that one must not let a thing like that get started.

* * * * *

47

I am at Amelia's chipped sink in the corner, washing the supper dishes with a cake of yellow soap, feeling my hands crack and grow red but sustained by the grateful wonderment Amelia and Gus must be feeling. They are in the living room with Becky, who is asleep in Gus's arms.

Gus grumbles something, which Amelia has to answer rather loudly because he's hard of hearing.

"You'd be out there washing those dishes, not holding that baby," she says, and I know he's complaining about my being here. He's saying they don't need me, he could have managed.

Could Gus be jealous of me? He is habitually and obsessively jealous of everybody else poor stiff prim virtuous Amelia comes near or even looks at, including Fred, but *me*? Not even Gus can be that crazy. He must be thinking of my laziness. He must mean he can't imagine any help I can be. I'll just be underfoot and befoul the house with cigarette smoke.

Exit Florence Nightingale. My conceit may be somewhat fragile.

But I'm here for Amelia, not Gus. I don't like him either. We're even. He can stand this if I can. And he does love Becky. That should help.

He adores Becky, and is constantly suspicious of her good health and good spirits. He keeps feeling her head for fevers and searching her eyes for glassiness. It's funny how Gus feels about Becky. He's not sure he's Fred's father, and he's damn sure Fred's not Becky's father, but Gus never for a moment doubts that he is Becky's grandfather. But I, alas, am her mother, so something has to go wrong.

Can I stand two weeks with Gus in this cold

bleak clean hard farm house? To be both unwelcome and uncomfortable! There's not a soft surface anywhere except the beds, and they're not very. The rest is iron and wood and linoleum, plus the hard lumpy scuffed-up leather couch someone else threw out. There's a coal stove in the living room and a kerosene cook stove in the kitchen. At least there's rudimentary electricity and a bathroom with hot water. Fred did that with his mustering-out pay when he got home from Germany in 1946 three years ago. Gus thinks it's all sissy nonsense. The barn's good enough for *him*, but of course he's just a plain man with no fancy degrees, no education at all except in the School of Root Hog or Die.

Amelia used to envy Gus and Fred the barn, all snug and toasty with its big warm cows. It doesn't seem warm to me, bone-rattling in fact, but Amelia says I should try a country backhouse. Then I'll think barns are warm. The bathroom doesn't seem like nonsense to her. I think Gus hates it because he couldn't give it to her. He wants to be the only one who gives her anything.

At dawn Gus goes to the barn, which is piteously below standard. He has six cows. By law, only the condensary is allowed to buy the milk. While he's out there, I'm supposed to get the coal fire going and make breakfast.

I succeed for a couple of mornings, at great emotional cost, but on the third morning I don't wake up until the back door slams. Gus is in the back room. I am cornered in my predicted unworthiness. I jump up, rush to the kitchen while struggling into my robe.

And there is the breakfast, ready on the stove, and poor invalid Amelia looking wonderfully just-up and inactive at the table. "We won't say anything to Gus," she murmurs, in a way that is simply amused and kind, not saintly. When Gus clumps in, I have the oatmeal pan in my hand, ready to dish up, and a glow in my heart that stays and stays.

It's like that every morning now, except that she calls me, gently, when she sees Gus start in from the barn. Once up, I work like a proper rural drudge and Amelia rests, just as she is supposed to. I feed the stove and carry out the ashes and deal with the dust the ashes make, and launder and make beds and wash dishes and cook. It amazes me how much of a day can be lost just in the processes that surround feeding when you try to do a good job. I start thinking about what to get for dinner (which is farmer for lunch) while washing the breakfast dishes and the milking machine. And then the peeling and sloshing around! It is cruel and unusual punishment.

I do work hard, but there's time to talk with Amelia too, while Gus is outside. He's getting old and slow so he takes a long time to do negligible work. The longer he takes the better we like it.

Can Amelia be mellowing toward me? She remembers now that she herself was once young and reading, letting the housework slide. So many times her in-laws caught her sitting with a book among the dirty dishes! The humiliation reformed her. "I resolved never to be caught like that again, and I haven't been," she tells me proudly, and I see in her face a quiet confidence that I will go and do likewise.

"But what about your reading?" I ask, resolving not to.

"Oh, I still find time for some."

She used to love Dickens and George Eliot and *The Autocrat of the Breakfast Table* and *Walden.* Now between supper dishes and bed with Gus, there's barely time to learn about the countries her church sends missionaries to and read 1/365 of the Bible a day.

Her face is so sweet when she looks at me. I could almost believe she likes me. She says, "I am realizing that God is not only just, but also merciful," and I know she consents to my not being damned to hell. Have my good intentions moved her? No, I think the existence of Becky has presented Amelia with a theological dilemma.

Her hideous church is very big on infant damnation. While I was pregnant she told me, "A child can't inherit salvation from a parent who doesn't have it, any more than he can inherit money." That made sense to her then. It was simply justice, tolerable for someone abstract, such as a fetus. But here's Becky, real as a tree, laughing a big open-mouthed laugh, showing her pink gums with the spaces marked off for teeth. No grandma could touch that realness and go on thinking infant damnation was a truly good idea. And if the only way to keep Becky out of hell is to keep me out, so be it.

I grew up in a religion exactly like Amelia's. I know all about it. It is grim and vile. My grandmother terrorized my childhood with it. My mother was too busy to notice. I lived in constant fear of the Second Coming, afraid to look at the sky lest I see the Cloud No Bigger Than A Man's Hand, which would become enormous, would be revealed as Jesus with His Heavenly Host come to open the graves, raise the dead, rescue the good and set fire to the rest of us, a fire in which we could not even die, in which we would burn forever. Grandma said she and I were good, of course. She didn't realize that I personally was a sinner. She said we would be safe on the Cloud with Jesus, looking down and laughing at my dad and all my relatives on his side of the family and Grandma's second husband on fire.

Thank God, so to speak, I was also taught that the Bible is the Infallible Word of God, "inerrant," the preacher liked to say, and he made no adjustment for metaphor, so if you can catch it in even one error you can pull the whole thing down. *Genesis* is a treasury of errors.

Fred was taught all that stuff too, of course, but it rolled right off him, thanks to Gus. Gus told him, "Now, Freddie, pay it no mind. Just you go along with it and keep your mouth shut. It's just a little something to keep the women quiet." As far as Amelia knows, Fred is saved. Can't Becky inherit salvation from him? Too risky! Salvation could depend on mothers only. Better to let God be merciful.

I am allowed to drive Gus's huge second-hand Pontiac, his first powerful car, six feet tall and heavy as a train, to town. He watches me back out of the barn as anxiously as if I were running off with his testicles. The car is so sluggish that I feel I'm dragging it with my gut, until the highway where I can hit sixty-five. Then it goes like a bird. Gus is so proud of this demon monster. Amelia hates it. She told me, "He drives sixty-five miles an hour on country roads, with his eyes on his neighbors' crops. There's no possible way for him not to have an accident." Worry about his life bores me. She bores me when, sometimes, she boasts of having kept Gus alive past the deaths of several of his younger brothers, despite his having been sickly when she married him. I want her to be brusquely human, and when she talked about Gus's inevitable accident she suddenly was. "I just wish I didn't have to be with him when it happens," she said, and she laughed with me, but not as hard.

I nudge the monster in beside a gas pump, like a ship's pilot berthing an ocean liner. The attendant comes out. "It wants more," I say.

"An old Silver Streak" he says. "Wonderful old car. It can pass anything except a gas station."

The tank seems bottomless, an abyss, but isn't quite. I hand over lots of Fred's money and go on my way to the frozen-food locker.

I bring out white-wrapped pieces of a cow that

Gus shot in the head and disemboweled and Amelia cut up and wrapped. She used to can their cows in dozens of two-quart Mason jars. Freezing is a recent luxury.

I bring too many white-wrapped packages back to the farm. One spoils. It just plain rots. This precious meat has more than hard work in it, it has grief too, for the cow that did her best for Gus for years, gave him calves and milk, trusted him. And I have let a piece of her rot. I am so ashamed. Trembling with guilt, I re-close the package.

Gus is asleep in his hard wooden rocking chair in the living room, but he has the keenest possible nose, from clean country living and never smoking. If I unwrap the meat and let the odor escape, his nose will wake him. There will be no hiding place. Waste enrages him. I don't like it either, but here I am.

There is nothing to do but take Amelia into my confidence. She hates waste too, but I have no choice. I whisper and beckon, get her to the kitchen, point at the limp package, hang my head. She doesn't hesitate. Noble woman! She seizes the package, carries it past the actual sleeping ogre, and flings it into the living room stove. Such expertise! Has she done this before? Gus snores on without missing a syllable.

So now Amelia and I have another secret. It moves us to a new level, warm, confidential. I am washing the breakfast dishes. Amelia stands at the kitchen window watching Gus clump to the barn.

"How would *you* like it," she asks with weary

loathing, not hotly, "having *that* love you and kiss you?"

"I couldn't stand it," I say.

"Well, I can't stand it either."

And she spends the day telling me stories she will probably soon regret. I think such openness is unprecedented for her. It must scare her to be talking at last, and to me of all people, her own daughter-in-law, a child, who is a completely unsuitable person and is trying to be a writer and doesn't have a discreet bone in her body. But when you tell your inner griefs to a writer, isn't there something in you wishing to leave a record, hoping that after you and your enemy are safely dead and nobody will be hurt, someone will know what you went through? Don't we all cry the cry of the ghost of Hamlet's father, *"Remember me, remember me!"*? Writers never forget and sooner or later will tell. Maybe something in her realizes this and makes her choose me.

I see Amelia's life. I see her mother, whose sisters all moved to Oklahoma when it opened up, but she couldn't go along because her husband refused. She lost her mother-power then, while Amelia was still a baby. A dear older sister, messy, always reading, raised Amelia. Gus won't let that sister in the house. "He thinks I love her better than him, and yes, I do." Kindly neighbors took Amelia to church. She was the only one in her family who cared for church.

I see shy gawky Amelia, always too tall, forcing herself not to slump, going off to teachers' college, becoming a country schoolmarm, catching the attention of a troll. He was the grown-up brother of

55

one of her pupils, a boy every other teacher had dismissed as stupid. He wasn't stupid, merely almost blind. Amelia spent extra time with him, uncovered his intelligence. His huge family loved her for that. They seemed to be a jolly family, full of jokes, always laughing, playing tricks on each other. They all had nicknames. They called Amelia "Mealy." She'd always wanted a nickname. They were excited because Gus was coming home from a year on the bum, seeing the country, bold free-spirited Gus. What tales he would bring them!

He set his will on Amelia. To get some room, she spent the summer in Oklahoma. Gus courted her from afar with chocolates every day in the mail. They arrived melted. Their being melted touched her. She loved Gus because his courtship was so awkward, and because he gave money to his mother when he needed it to start his own life. Too late, Amelia found out Gus hated his mother for whining until she got his money. "Bloodsucker! Vampire!" he raged, too late.

Amelia married without knowing there was such a thing as sexual intercourse, as good women did then, and never got used to the invasion and indignity and dailyness and mess of it. She had to get rid of the semen stench without a bathroom, and sometimes Gus told her she smelled and made him smell. He thought she smelled from her own natural female dirtiness. "Well, I never smelled until I married him," she says. She ordered spermicidal jelly from the Sears, Roebuck catalog, so Fred was the only child. Gus wanted more children, jolly and bold like him, not studious and grammatical and careful like Fred and Amelia. "You want a nickel, Freddie?" he'd ask. "No," Fred would say, because he knew how few nickels there were. "Freddie, you was born an old man," Gus would say. Sometimes Amelia thinks Gus is still trying for another child, a miracle menopause son. Why else does he persist? "You'd think someone who can hardly get across the room anymore could be through with that too," she says.

She asked her doctor if this much activity was normal. Were all men like Gus? She had no way of knowing and no one else to ask. "No, they're not," the doctor said, "but they'd like to be. You are one lucky lady!"

One of the triumphs of Gus's unresting imagination has been the belief in female lust, which led naturally to the belief that Amelia must be doing something very clever about hers. Amelia was surprised and hurt when the doctor, not a crazy bumpkin but an educated man, also believed in female lust.

Amelia's teaching supported the family during the Great Depression. She gave her pay to Gus, who doled a little of it back, suspiciously. One winter he did let her buy Fred his first new jacket. Once she let some jelly she was making burn black. (Just brown they would have eaten.) She had to eat her oatmeal without sugar until she made up the loss. "I *hate* oatmeal without sugar," she says.

He thinks he's a successful farmer who makes a good living, and the only reason they're poor is because Amelia is wasteful and gullible, handing out cash by the fistful to anybody with a hard-luck story.

She had, and still has, terrible long-lasting nauseating headaches, and intestinal spasms like labor pains. She can't sleep. Every dawn from spring to winter, she hears the birds begin. When Fred was away at war, she slept a few nights in his bed, easily, sweetly, but Gus was jealous. It must have seemed incestuous. Anyway, he can't sleep without her. Sometimes she wants to scream and sob the way her mother did, but can stop herself by praying.

Furiously I ask, "Why is it more important for him to sleep than for you to?"

"It's all right," Amelia says. "God gives me the strength whenever I ask Him for it."

Neither church nor state would find anything objectionable in this marriage.

I say, "You don't have to stay. You don't have to live this way."

"I have to stay where it has pleased God to place me."

She begins trying to take everything back, saying, "Oh, it's not so bad. Oh, it's all right, I guess. I've become accustomed to it."

There are many admirable things about Gus, she says. She was unfair to leave them out. He is so courageous, so tough and uncomplaining, so independent, unmooching.

I say, "Yes, it takes some courage for a third-grade dropout to court a college graduate."

"Oh, that! It wouldn't be his way to feel a woman could be above him. And of course we have God's word: 'The man is the head of the woman, as Christ is the head of the man.' It didn't take all that much courage. I mean other things. The way he upbraids the banker. The way he believes he's six feet tall. The way he sits down and thinks when he has a problem to solve, instead of running around in a panic. To me that is admirable."

"To me too," I say, but I am already plotting rescue. She should be near the people she loves, Fred and Becky and — me? She should be able to sleep alone. I have to find a way to make that happen.

Gus has gone to bed. Amelia steals a minute before she must go too. She stands facing me.

"I'm letting him think I don't care for you, but I do," she says, and gives me a full warm hug and a lingering kiss on the cheek. "You remind me of my sister. You're good for my Fred. You build him up."

Every night and morning now she embraces me the same way, and every night I lie in bed remembering her hug and kiss, weeping but not unhappy, instead very happy, feeling my heart be born.

Something very authentic, unmistakable, divinely correct, takes possession of me. It sweeps away my icy caution, my fear of icily cautious women, my fear of pain. I will love women. I will go openhearted at whatever cost. I will not push Becky away, and if she grows up knowing she needs women, well, how beautiful!

* * * * *

Amelia and Gus are visiting us. They drove down

in the immortal Silver Streak. We see them rarely now that we've moved so far away. They're too old to travel, and we have too many children to travel. We are participating in the Baby Boom.

Fred has taken Gus to work with him. Amelia and I are alone at the dining table with all our history between us, silencing us. The two years we all lived together in a big duplex house, my failed rescue of her, her failed reform of me, all stand between us, thick with embarrassment and guilt.

When good example didn't work, she used her in-laws' methods on me. She believed in them because they'd worked on her, but I could be ashamed of myself to the verge of suicide without reforming. I wondered whether Amelia was trying to drive me away, in the illusion that Fred and the children wouldn't come with me, that she could have Fred back with a bonus.

I know she's sorry. I know she lies awake nights being sorry. She is so sorry she can't speak of it.

I lured her and Gus off the farm, into a duplex, and left them to find a tenant for our half. I am so sorry I can't speak of it.

We sit not looking at each other, drinking our coffee. I am thinking how we got wrecked on the mighty rock of love, our different beliefs about love. I believed that if she loved me she would accept me more or less as I was. She believed that if I loved her I would want to become like her. So it didn't take either of us long to feel unloved.

The children run in breathlessly, gulp water, run back to their games, their little pals. Grandma's visit doesn't excite them. All they wanted was to open the gifts she brought them, striped terrycloth bathrobes she made on her foot-powered Singer sewing machine. The kids did thank her politely, but they really wanted toys. She knows that. So the failure of her strenuous gifts is between us too.

"I want to read you something," I say, a risk I suddenly want to take. I go to my study, bring out my notebook. I pretend my handwriting is too illegible even for her, old master teacher, old cryptanalyst who can decipher anything. I have to read it to her. The fact is, I don't want to see her face while she takes this in, lest I stop it half way. I read:

I would have raised my kids unlovingly — unphysically, that is — if Becky and I hadn't gone to the farm for those two weeks that first winter of her life. I fell in love with my mother-in-law and longed for her hug and kiss. Lying under all those handmade quilts, thinking of Amelia with full exalted love, I knew I could give Becky full access to my body and heart and bed. Faith in love came over me then. Where once my whole effort had been to hide my love, I then began to want to show it, to want the points at which it could be demonstrated. I knew with full firmness that the lack of somebody like Amelia in my life was what had ailed me. Achieving her, and giving myself to be that in the lives of other women, became my driving ambition.

I stop reading. I hold my notebook up to hide my

face. I dare not look at Amelia. She is silent for a long time.

"To think," she says at last, "that all the while I was longing for the same thing."

Now I can look at her, see her blushes, her tears, and show her mine.

Now the words can come. "I'm sorry ..." we say. "I thought ..." "I realize ..." Everything is sayable, easy. "I love ..." "I feel ..." We even laugh. The past is transformed.

The children come in. Fred and Gus come in. My lover Beth drops by on her way home from work to pay her respects to Amelia. Never before have I been sorry to see Beth. She is courteous, conventional, playing well-brought-up young woman to respected elder. Then she says, "I have to run."

"Just a minute. I want to show you something," I say, and lead her to the basement, the only unpeopled space left in the house. I say, "I want to show you a kiss," and kiss her.

"That's what I came to see," she says.

Beth drives off whistling in her little blue car. Amelia and I, our great conversation now impossible, start cooking. Who's this clumping up the basement stairs? Gus! How long was he down there? How much did he see?

Everything, I guess. I don't really care. What can he do? Tell Fred? Fred already knows. On his way through the kitchen Gus says, "We'll be leaving first thing tomorrow. Don't want to wear out our welcome." Now I know what he can do.

"All right, Gus," Amelia calls after him.

"No!" I say. "Not when we just got so we can talk! We've just barely begun!"

She smiles and shakes her head.

"*Resist him!*" I say. "He's not your master. You *know* you're welcome. You *know* you haven't stayed too long."

She smiles and shakes her head. " 'The man is the head of the woman as Christ is the head of the man,' " she says.

That night I dream I am on a train with a big limp woman, like a rag doll, who tips over whenever I don't hold her up. Someone says it must be hard for me, being with her, having her dependent on me. I say, in German so she won't understand, "In drei Wochen wird sie tot sein." In three weeks she will be dead.

I wake up scared.

I am at my desk. It's the middle of the night. Far away the phone rings. Fred comes to my study door. He is crying. "That was Pa. Ma's had a stroke. I have to go."

Weeping, I help him pack. "I didn't thank her for my birthday present," I say. "Tell her I like it."

"I will," Fred sobs.

There will be times when I persist in love past all reason, forgive rebuff, keep trying. Never again, I swear it on my mother's breasts, will someone not know I love her until three weeks before she dies.

TILDY

Tildy was picking strawberries in her bathing suit to get a tan, not that she would, not that she ever did. Her skin was incurably white, except for the red V at her throat, which was the accumulation of years. Many years. She was forty-one. The bathing suit was from Sears, black (the other choice had been royal blue) and despite being the biggest Sears offered, it didn't quite cover both bottom and breasts. She had to keep choosing which direction to pull it, not that it mattered so far from the road and no near neighbors.

The picking was tiring because the strawberry plants had escaped their rows and made a solid leafy mass. She didn't want to crush any of them, so she couldn't sit or kneel but had to step carefully, nudging a clear foothold, and then bend from the hips. That was good for her, she knew, and would have the bathing suit fitting in no time.

She rested whenever she wanted to and ate the red berries, pushed them up against the roof of her mouth and broke them with her tongue. Dead ripe, warm from the sun, and so sweet. They looked like red-faced blond men who needed a shave. Could she make a poem of that, maybe a sort of humorous poem for a farm journal which would pay, surely, at least ten dollars? She didn't want much money, just a little to show some people her poetry wasn't useless.

Since she was lying on the ground, resting, she felt the car in her driveway before she heard it. Then its door slammed. She rolled over and looked toward her house. The girl was pounding on her door and shouting. Not "Yoo-hoo!" the way a normal person would, but "Tildy! Tildy!"

Tildy decided not to answer, because of the bathing suit, which the girl would like too much. What a funny embarrassing thing this all was!

The girl kept shouting, walking around the house. She was so pregnant she almost waddled. She made Tildy a little sad, like a dog at its master's grave. In many ways, she was a nice girl. A very nice girl. Or she had been at the beginning anyway, warm and bright and clever. She made Tildy laugh and feel smart at the beginning. Feel almost wise, and certainly wonderful. But now, "Tildy! Tildy!" she kept shouting, and that was annoying. Anyone else would see Tildy wasn't home and just go on.

Tildy turned her face, not to have to watch that pitiful circling of her house anymore. She laid her head down on her straw hat and might even have dozed a little, if there hadn't been ants crawling on her, and then she felt a tiny vibration in the ground and opened her eyes. The girl was sitting watching her.

"You're awake!" the girl said.

Tildy shook her head as though to clear it of sleep. "If you say so," she said.

"I can't stay long. Don't worry."

"I'm not worried. I never worry."

"You're looking wonderful." (That damned little suit that wouldn't stay up or down!)

Tildy stood up, pulled the suit over her bottom, held the hat over her front, and went toward her house.

"May I come in?"

"I don't think you'd better."

"I'm terribly tired. I won't stay."

"I want to put some clothes on."

"Go ahead."

Tildy put her robe on. She'd made it herself out of old drapes. She went back outside.

The girl said, "I like your robe. I like your chair you upholstered yourself with awning cloth. I like your house. And your pans. And your little elephants pointing east. And everything about you. I like your husband and your children. And your jalopy. And your poems. And your little house that's full of love."

"Start liking your *own* house and husband and children. They're nice too."

"It doesn't work that way. This is a vale of tears, haven't you noticed? I want to be reborn as a

67

neglected child. I'll be barefoot in the snow and the social worker will bring me to you."

She was beyond anything Tildy could imagine. Nothing in life, nothing in a story, had ever hinted there could be someone like this girl. A mother who wanted a mother?

Tildy said nothing. She decided to start hulling the berries, to keep busy. The girl said, "I wanted to ask you."

Tildy, saying nothing, hulled a berry with a neat little nip that snatched the green star off and flicked it away.

"If you'll come see me in the hospital."

"Hospital?"

"When I have the baby."

"How will I know?"

"I'll phone you."

"You? How can you phone me?"

"Afterward. I'll go to a pay phone in the hall and phone you. Will you come?"

"I can't promise. It might not be convenient."

The girl was mute at last. She stood with her head bent, glowering through her eyebrows at Tildy, who sat nipping the berries and not looking back.

Finally the girl said. "He's promised we can move away. It isn't as though you'd be starting anything again."

Someone hearing that "again" would think there *was* something before.

Had anyone in the world ever made so much of one kiss, one little kiss — two at the most — given in friendship and curiosity? Tildy wished she could understand, but whenever she thought about it something inside her got nervous. The main thing to remember was to stay away from funny stuff, not play with it. Plain life was complicated enough.

"I *told* you, it might not be convenient," Tildy said.

"Oh God! Oh God, I'm scared! Of what will happen to me. You know how having a child shakes you up. Even when you go into it happy and calm. What will it be this time? I'm scared what it will do to me this time. When I feel like this ahead of time."

"Are you trying to tell me something?"

"*Yes,* for God's sake, you stupid bitch!"

And the girl rushed, as well as she could, all cumbersome and awkward, down the slant of grass, past the flowerbed, to her car and away.

Tildy knew the girl would be all right. This was just a little insanity of pregnancy. Her husband loved her. Her children would keep her busy and pull her back into plain life.

THE OUTSIDER

Daddy said he couldn't spare the cash right then for plane fare.

I said I'd spend my own.

Lee Ann said it wasn't quite spending my *own* if she and Daddy had to replace it, now was it? She said I keep forgetting I'm only one member of a large family.

I said I don't forget it.

Lee Ann said it seemed to her I'd had just a *bit* more than my share, what with my orthodontist and my contact lenses and not getting a scholarship, and now the shrink, and she would be pretty much in favor of washing her hands of me if I couldn't stay away from my mother, considering who it was that messed me up and made me not study hard enough to get a scholarship, and who made me need the shrink. ("Your therapist," she calls him.)

"If you like your mother so much, go live with her," Lee Ann said. "I wish you would. Let *her* pay for your therapist. She's the one who should. Let her lady friend pay for your therapist, I mean, *excuse* me. I realize she can't, herself. She can only *make* problems, not do anything about them."

I just kept quiet and hated her and concentrated on having all my hate show.

Daddy said, "All right, Rebecca, that's enough."

I was going to run up to my room and slam the door, the way I always did before. But then I remembered I don't *have* a room anymore. It's the nursery for the new baby.

So then I was going to jump on my bike that Mother bought me when I was ten. She said someday I could go hosteling across Europe on it and take it to college. She always gave me everything too soon — before I was ready for it. Who when they're ten needs a black English gear-shift touring bike? But I grew up to it and lots of times I zoomed off into the night on it when I couldn't stand Lee Ann anymore and she couldn't stand me, and Daddy let me do it because he had to keep on the good side of Lee Ann. He runs this whole marriage scared, afraid to fail again. And Lee Ann wouldn't be nice about everything the way Mother was. Lee Ann would clean him out, and he knows it.

But my bike was up at school. So I took Emily's out of the garage. I knew she wouldn't mind. She likes me. She really does. It's crazy. All I've ever done since we were little is boss her around and tease her and kick her out of games, but she really likes me. She's spineless. She's a real goody-goody Pollyanna type, and she's got 20/20 eyes, the whole bit. She's never had anything but A's in school, she's a natural for a Presidential Merit Award, she's always cleaning and helping and being sweet to people and making everybody think she's beautiful and wonderful. She won't cost a cent dentally or mentally or educationally, and she's really crazy about me. She should be. I really make her look good. She just makes me sick. She got along with Mother, and now she gets along with Lee Ann, and she's nice to all the little kids, and I knew she wouldn't mind a bit if I took her bike.

I was just pushing it down the driveway when Lee Ann came out on the porch and asked whose bike *is* that? She was going to explain again about respect for property, so I just threw my leg over and took off. I felt, I think, a lot the way Mother used to when she backed her car out and roared away. I just wanted to go and go, and get real tired.

I felt so *lonesome,* because Daddy didn't dare to be on my side anymore and always stuck up for Lee Ann, even when she was *saying* nasty things and I was merely *looking* nasty, and because Mother may be fun and interesting, but Lee Ann's right — Mother really can't take care of anybody and I couldn't have a room of my own if I went there either. She's not making any money anymore. The stuff she writes since the divorce nobody will publish. She just *deliberately* writes things she knows no one will publish, and keeps house for Vera and Vera supports her and they're Lesbians in Greenwich Village. And that's what the shrink and I talk about — and also if I am too, and we think probably not, because I truly enjoy boys a lot but on the other hand I could be kidding myself. So Lee Ann's right — Mother, through me, is costing Lee Ann and Daddy a lot of money, but also Mother earned an awful lot when she was writing what people liked and one of her books was even a movie, and when she and Vera went away, all Mother took was her filing cabinet and some books. She didn't even take her car. Vera had one.

So I was riding Emily's bike as fast as I could, heading nowhere special. The starlings were cawing away. Early evening. Pretty soon there'd be fireflies, and fireflies always make me feel so awful unless I'm with somebody I really love a lot. I'd missed the sunset, or the best of it, trying to get plane fare to Mother. There's this hill west of town I like to climb every night to watch the sunset over the lake. It sounds corny, but practically every night, unless I had play rehearsal, or I had to put some last-minute touches on the school paper, I used to climb up that hill and watch the sunset until the evening star came out and then I'd wish on the evening star and go home. I wished for love. I told Mother about it last summer, and she said the evening star is usually Venus, and love is exactly what Venus should be prayed to for.

I was wondering whether to try for the last of the sunset when I heard bike wheels, and it was Daddy, on *Rosemary's* bike. Like Lee Ann said, we're a big family. Our garage looks like a bike factory. The cars have to stay out in the weather.

Daddy handed me a flashlight and I put it into the clip and we rode along not looking at each other. I was afraid he'd look silly and try to make me laugh, him with his long legs on a little girl's bike with the seat way low. I used to think he was so amusing. So wonderful and silly. Or else he'd try to get into a heart-to-heart talk, starting, "How are you, Becky?" I just hate it when he says, in that awful *earnest* way, "How are you, Becky?" He used to say that a lot after Mother went away, before he got all wrapped up in Lee Ann.

But he didn't say anything and we just rode along, and all of a sudden I knew he was missing Mother too.

I'm very good at knowing what people are thinking. Like one time, Mother was standing at the sink looking out the window, and I just knew, and I said, "What are you admiring?" And actually she had no real expression at all. She said, "Just daydreaming," but I ran to another window and looked out and saw a pretty lady in a purple dress walking along with her butt kind of gently jiggling. I was about five then. I never forget anything, either, and that was one of the things I put together to figure out about Mother and Vera. Also a little while after Vera started coming around our house, I dreamed that Mother and Daddy got divorced. I tell you I *know* things. All except what *I* am and what I'm supposed to do and what's going to happen to me.

So I knew Daddy was missing Mother, and feeling bad because there wasn't one single person he could admit it to. Grownups don't seem to have any friends. I mean, people they really talk with. I don't see how they stand it, keeping everything inside, and just talking about the ballgame or the garden. To me, friendship is practically the most important thing, and I have quite a few very good friends except they all go to Europe or somewhere every summer. But I know all their secrets and they know mine. They know all about Mother and Vera, and which boys I've let do it, and I know all about who's got a grandmother in a mental hospital, and whose very bigshot father tried to murder his whole family, and whose mother is drunk every afternoon, and who's bedding down with who. Which boys love boys, which girls love girls. I mean, our whole group, everybody knows everything like that. And it all seems kind of natural and human, and you don't look down on anybody and it's all easy.

But grownups. I really have to think they don't know very much about life. I know that sounds like what kids always think, but it's really true. And how can they know anything, when they never really tell each other anything and never read anything? Like, Daddy reads *Time* and his professional journals, and the newspaper. Lee Ann reads *Cosmopolitan* and stuff like that — because Daddy didn't want "another intellectual woman, that's for sure" — so they thought if I had to be yelled at to clean my room or do my homework, they had some huge awful problem like nobody ever had in the world before.

Mother left the house just crammed with wonderful books, but they're all in boxes in the basement now, getting mildewy. I've spent quite a lot of time down there reading them. Emily's getting so she wants to, too, but I sock her and won't let her. I tell her Mother specifically stated that Emily was not to use these books. I'm so mean to Emily and she keeps liking me. She's crazy. But I don't see why Emily or *any*body else should, for instance, see Mother's poetry books — Edna St. Vincent Millay and Elinor Wylie and all — and see what she underlined and the little remarks she wrote in the margins when she was younger than I am now. When I see the young dumb things she used to say, I feel like I have to protect her.

And anyway, Emily gets along with Lee Ann. She doesn't have a right to Mother, while she's getting along with Lee Ann.

Well, I knew Daddy was missing Mother, and wanting to talk about her. I knew he wouldn't bring her up, and I almost felt sorry enough for him to bring her up myself. It's really pitiful, how even when I got back from seeing Mother last summer he didn't ask me anything about her, and how bored and wrapped up in his newspaper or TV he tried to act if I said anything about her, with his ears practically in points and practically sending out beeps.

I rode along wondering if I was madder or sorrier at him. He really did let me down, whenever it was between me and Lee Ann, even though back when it was me and Mother fighting he was always on my side. Did he have a right to hear about Mother, when he never took her side when he had her here? I thought this way and that way, and finally I decided to say, "Mother's hair's getting real gray," and said it.

He just stopped pedaling and when I turned to see where he was, he was turning around and heading home with his knees sticking out like oars. I didn't mean to hit him that hard.

I thought I might follow, but the same reason I had to go out was still in force, and made it so I couldn't go back. I didn't live there anymore. The trouble was, I didn't live anyplace else either.

So I decided I'd go see Tammy and stay the night with her, even though her mother's real afraid Tammy's a Lesbian and makes everybody sleep apart and it wouldn't be any fun. Tammy was the only girlfriend I had that wasn't away for the summer. Otherwise I wouldn't have gone there, because her mother's right, Tammy is a Lesbian about me. Last spring I kissed her, and I didn't get much out of it, but Tammy fell in love with me.

Like I knew she would be, Tammy was real glad to see me in a sappy foolish way, like no poise at all and this little kiddish nervous giggle, and she's my age, she's seventeen, there's no excuse for that. I don't mean I don't like her. I like her a lot. Just not the way she wishes I did.

And it felt good to be welcomed somewhere, except by her mother, who never let us out of her sight except to go to the bathroom once. While she was gone I gave Tammy a quick kiss with some tongue-tip, because it was such fun to see her blush. She has this very thin pink skin. Add a blush to that, and it's like she's bleeding.

I wrote to Mother about kissing Tammy, thinking she might be pleased, but she gave me hell, a little, and told me not to mess around with sincere people until I felt sincere myself. I could see whose side she was on in *that*. Tammy always said, even before she knew why, that she wished she had my mother instead of her own. And I think Mother would have been glad right then to have Tammy instead of me as her daughter.

STRANGERS IN CAMELOT

I am sure that people are always telling you
their stories with the proud announcement, "My life
would make a wonderful book — the trouble is
nobody would believe it." Well, I am no exception,
Miss Miller, except that it isn't exactly my own story
I am going to tell you, but one that has been
brought to my attention. But the one whose story it
is knows I am writing to you, in the hope that you
will see fit to turn what I say into a smoother form,
because it is in some ways an important story, and
very topical, and to us at least very interesting.

I think firstly, you need to make the time of the
story very clear. That is, not give the impression

that it took place back in the McCarthy Period which we are all so glad is over. The time is 1961, right now, so to speak, during the administration of John Kennedy and his adorable children. The place is Washington, D.C. You may want to describe the lovely parks and trees and statues to give some atmosphere, also the beautiful Potomac. There is something charming about the way the avenues run diagonal and at their intersections have little round parks with statues of General Thomas or General Scott on their horses. You could say something like "prancing horses" if you'd like to use more active words, but I leave that entirely to your capable hands.

The main character is a more-or-less young woman. I will not describe her, since I am sure you can make up an appearance that will have appeal to readers. I will only say that she is not in her first youth, and that she is somewhat on the plain side. Perhaps, considering the story, I should also explain that she is reasonably feminine in appearance and manner, and that she readily makes friends with people of both sexes and all ages, as well as animals. I mean, please don't present her as a dried-up bitter "old maid" whom nobody likes. She has a warm, fresh, uncritical attitude towards people, and understands why they make mistakes and doesn't scold or complain. Well, I am sure I am making her sound "goody-goody," which is misleading too. She is a warm, loving, generous, open-hearted, wonderful person, but she can get cross too, or depressed or discouraged just like anybody else, I assure you! Her name is Miss X, and she is (or was) employed as a Civil Servant by the Fish and Wildlife

Service of the Department of the Interior, in an administrative capacity. (I trust that you will find an adequate disguise for this, such as Tree and Flora Service of the Department of Agriculture, or perhaps it would be simplest just to say that she works for Department X in the office of the Secretary of X. (Since I am calling her X, it begins to look like nepotism, doesn't it!) You should make it absolutely clear that she is not a typist or clerk, that she is a woman of high education and ability, working in an administrative capacity, though not the highest. She is a GS-13, if that would mean anything to your readers.

I should also add that she has nothing whatever to do with National Defense, Cuba policy, the appointment of ambassadors, outer space, and so on. You may have to mention Fish and Wildlife Service after all, to make that clear, or something equivalent.

Nevertheless she is subject to a security check, like every other Government employee. This means that she has to fill out a quite long form, listing every place she has lived since she left her parental home, and give the names of two people who knew her in each city. Then the investigators, using this list, go to the people she knew in her (by now) fairly long life and fairly many travels, and they ask about her politics and whether she drinks to excess and her erotic life. I am trying to write this very plainly and not act indignant, but I think you as an artist would know how to give it some drama, and make your readers understand how painful it would be to have your old friends and neighbors asked these questions about you, even if your life is an open book, as hardly any life is, particularly in the erotic area.

Well, that is the case with Miss X. Politically and regarding alcohol, she has a very fine history, but erotically there are some difficulties.

It is perhaps idle to speculate on what put the investigators "on the trail" of a certain person who, to this day, bears a great malice towards Miss X. Perhaps some old neighbor mentioned a frequent associate. Perhaps Miss X's medical history (which she is also required to write out for the investigators in full) which includes a period of psychotherapy, makes them look particularly hard for this certain person. You will never guess, Miss Miller, where they found her: in a mental hospital, Miss Miller, that's where.

(This story would be interesting from the point of view of the investigators too, Miss Miller. How glad they must be that their witnesses don't have to stand any test of credibility or competence!)

I will call this old enemy Miss A, to put her at the other end of the alphabet entirely. So here is Miss A (could you make a scene of this?) perhaps rocking on the screened-in porch of her ward in the mental hospital, and the attendant comes up and says, "Some gentlemen to see you, Miss A." Well, you build up the scene, as only you know how. I kind of hate to think about it myself. Make Miss A about Miss X's age. Make her pretty, even, if you want to. The main thing is, she is a woman scorned, and "Hell hath no fury" like hers, and she tells the investigators many things, some false and some true. (Because Miss X did not scorn her quite soon enough, and a number of the things Miss A says are quite true.)

In case your readers might feel secure, thinking that no Government employee has anything to hide in his or her erotic life, and that all the "bad apples" are efficiently ferreted out, you might emphasize that Miss A, being committed, is a special case. She has nothing to lose in the line of career or reputation, and much to gain in the line of revenge, and most Government employees don't have a witness quite like her in their background.

Actually, I am getting ahead of my story. Miss X knows nothing of this. She only knows that her security clearance does not come through. She would like to buy a house. She would like to know whether she has a job and whether she will be staying in Washington. She goes to her Section Chief and asks him to ask the investigators whether they are going to clear her.

A day passes. The Section Chief comes to Miss X's office. "Oh, by the way, I would not buy that house if you ask me," he says. (You can touch up the conversation, I will not be offended.)

In fact, I think I will not attempt to reproduce the actual words. It is harder than it seems at first. I will merely summarize: he says that he should not be telling her this, but the FBI people have turned up a certain Miss A and they are very worried about what she told them. He says that the security regulations are very specific. He makes a joke about how the Russians could blackmail her into giving them some fish. He says that he personally would not care even if what Miss A claims is true. Make this sound sincere, Miss Miller, because it is. Emphasize that Miss X feels a real friendship and niceness extended by the Section Chief. It would be all too easy to make him sound false.

This is one of the first unexpected interesting things about this story: that the Section Chief becomes Miss X's friend when he learns of her history.

Miss X explains that Miss A is in that hospital. She asks that Miss A's testimony be disregarded.

"You're living with a woman now," the Section Chief says.

"Her!" she says, hoping to sound amazed. Because he is right in his interpretation of what this means.

Which brings me to yet another character, Miss Y, who lives, quietly, with Miss X.

When Miss X gets home that evening, she holds her finger over her lips and hands Miss Y the following note:

Say nothing. The apartment is probably bugged.

"Shall we go for a drive and pick up some dinner somewhere?" she asks loudly, for the Listeners. She takes back the note and adds to it: *The car could be bugged too.*

They walk in a park beside the Potomac. Find a good place, Miss Miller, to explain that the quiet park is a mistake. The Listeners can very easily focus their listening devices there. The train station with its confusion of many voices and noises would have been the right place to go. Do put this information in, people do need to know it, even though it is awkward and may not fit in naturally anywhere and could interrupt the beautiful easy flow of your writing.

Miss X, feeling that it is at last safe to talk, reports everything her Section Chief said, including his final remark, to wit: "Couldn't you get a gentleman friend or something?" She interprets this to mean that a gentleman friend would be taken note of, which is to say she is being watched and listened to.

She also tells Miss Y to burn her diaries and her "special" literature, but it is harder than you may think to do that in a city apartment. Putting them down the incinerator chute would not at all assure their being promptly burned. *And* Miss Y finds that she does not wish to burn her diaries, which serve her as a way of keeping track of herself, a sort of inexpensive "psychotherapy," and there are many things in them that she hopes to understand better when she reads them again in future years. She finds that she would rather be driven out of Washington in disgrace than give them up.

As for Miss X, she in her turn finds that she would rather be disgraced and unemployed than find a gentleman friend, even a make-believe one, or "beard," as so many hiding women do. This is the second unexpected interesting thing: she realizes that Miss Y means more to her than worldly success or the "plaudits of the masses," or the Ph.D. she has been so proud of and may now lose the benefit of. She boasts to the Listeners, if they are really there, and to Miss Y, that she is a very good typist and makes a fine cup of coffee and she can become somebody's "crackerjack" secretary in the Deep South if need be.

Everything they say is for the Listeners. You can hurry past the conversation here, Miss Miller. It is basically about how absurd any doubts about their "normality" are, and much about household concerns in the hope that the Listeners will be very bored, but you needn't bore your readers by repeating it. Your readers certainly aren't accustomed to being bored!

Miss Y takes pleasure in entertaining the Listeners by singing during household chores such misleading songs and ballads as "Oh My Man I Love Him So!" "He's My Guy," "Happiness Is Just a Thing Called Joe," "What More Can a Woman Do?" "Bill," "Woman Needs Man and Man Must Have His Mate," and et cetera. The Listeners are her first real audience, in case they *are* real, and she fancies they will tell their friends in "Show Biz" about her!

Sometimes when Miss X is late in getting home, because she works overtime more than anyone should have to, and the buses are slowed by traffic "jams" and ice and snow, which Washington never expects and therefore doesn't provide for, and the early-falling nights of winter have long ago fallen and still no Miss X's key in the door, Miss Y tells herself, "Don't worry, the Listeners won't let anybody 'mug' her!" This is what Miss Y tells herself, but she is not so sure!

Well, the above is a little effort to convey such parts of the experience as are somewhat positive.

In fact, the Misses X and Y are slowly losing their minds. All demonstrations of affection, which have been an important part of their well-being, have stopped. Their home, which has been joyful and intelligent, is now full of inane chatter — because what would the Listeners suspect them of doing during a silence?

88

Any real communication is achieved by writing with a ballpoint pen on bathroom tissue, which is then easily flushed away. "If the Listeners are checking the sewers, they are welcome to all they can eat," Miss X wrote once. One of her few humorous messages.

The building superintendent, or "super," who originally liked them so much that she actually said, "I am realizing it is not necessary to be mean to everybody," now scowls and turns away when the Misses X and Y greet her.

One evening in the elevator there is a man to whom someone else exclaims, "Oh, you are back again!" and the man shifts and mumbles. "Which apartment do you have now?" this Someone queries. The man replies, "Seventh floor," a strange thing to say in a six-story building, and that night Miss Y writes squares and squares of bathroom tissue about how that man is obviously "their cop" — he even resembles Miss Y's father, who was also a "cop" but much larger. "He is a nice man," she writes, "like my Dad — nice to everybody but me!" This may or may not be an example of how the Misses X and Y are losing their minds. It is somewhat "iffy," perhaps.

A clearer example may be in their car battery, which begins "dying" although the car is new and from a reputable manufacturer. Frequently it requires a "jump" to start, and one evening in a rainstorm and a traffic "jam" with the headlights, windshield wipers, and radio all putting stress on it, the battery suddenly expires. While waiting for the tow truck, our friends (for I hope I have persuaded you to like them, Miss Miller!) are bombarded by many unkind epithets and remarks as well as the unceasing "tooting" of car horns. In fact, some of the epithets refer, quite by chance, to the very aberration of which Miss X stands accused! But this is beside the point.

The point is that in their newly-acquired insanity, our friends believe the Listeners have connected "bugs" to the car battery and drained it. That night Miss X writes an eloquent bathroom tissue note about the injustice of having to buy a new battery to supply one's enemies with the means to destroy one. She appeals to the Constitutional protection against self-incrimination, but I am sure if she were able to keep her note and re-read it later in tranquility, she herself would acknowledge a trace of madness in it.

One last incident: an old and dear friend of Miss X's, someone with whom she has been on the warmest of terms in the past, now behaves in a very nervous, hasty, and unwelcoming manner when telephoned. She reluctantly says yes, the Misses X and Y may drop by, but when they stop their car in front of her house in Arlington, she rushes out, not to greet them but to return some borrowed books and say that she has an unexpected obligation and goodbye!

Our friends do not for a moment consider that this friend could have some perfectly reasonable explanation. For instance, as an Army major, this woman could have been put on some secret "alert" that she could not reveal. But their anxiety-warped minds instantly take the whole incident as proof that the Listeners are everywhere and that the major *knows* they are. Knows they know every move our friends make and write down the names of everybody they see. Please present this as sympathetically as possible, even though it is very marginal, sanitywise.

Now comes a great scene, Miss X being questioned by downy-cheeked youths from the FBI. They are dressed in dark suits. Miss X wears a knitted nylon dress striped red and navy blue, and sensible shoes. (She has a touch of gout in her big toe sometimes.) Well, I am not going to do your work for you, Miss Miller. I am giving you this story, and not even asking for a percentage, but *you* have to write it. (Please take this in the jocular spirit in which it is intended.)

Miss X, thanks to her Section Chief's insistence and his having friends in high places, is actually being allowed to know what she is accused of, and *who* said it. Actual names and places, out of her FBI file, are being given to her, as they just never are in general, usually, and how embarrassed these young lads are to be asking someone who reminds them of their mothers to confirm or deny the wild accusations that spewed from the angry lips of Miss A in the mental hospital. I cannot bring myself to specify, but some of the general topics are: coerced erotic acts, imprisonment, enslavement, brainwashing, witchcraft, and then, as hearsay, child molestation. All these Miss X is able quite truthfully and convincingly to deny, and if Miss A had been the FBI's only informant, Miss X would probably be at the Fish and Wildlife Service to this day.

But, alas, a certain Miss B, an admired professor to whom Miss X confided her doubts and fears early in life, also spoke to the FBI, no doubt having been assured that Miss X would never know anything about it, and Miss B is respectable and sane — in her way. Not all of her opinions are models of clear thinking and good sense, but they are, alas, central and widely held. To me she is as mad as Miss A, but I am trying to keep myself out of this.

At the mention of Miss B, Miss X begins to weep, overcome by the pain of the betrayal. Then how those awkward lads scurry for coffee and Coca-Cola to soothe her! How they apologize!

"Miss B misinterpreted the natural confusions of adolescence," sobs Miss X.

"I'm sorry. You were twenty-seven."

"I was retarded."

"I see you're Phi Beta Kappa. I'm sorry."

That should be enough to give you the flavor.

They offer her a lie-detector test, as a means of leaving "no stone unturned." She says those tests are unreliable, and refuses.

And so her security clearance is denied, but she continues to work at her job a little longer. Her Section Chief wants her departure to be orderly. Although now officially an "Enemy of the People," she works as much overtime as before, and even has to go in on Christmas Day, though that doesn't matter now because she has no guests for Christmas dinner and only Miss Y is inconvenienced.

One morning Miss X stays home sick with a flareup of gout. Her Section Chief telephones her, to say he has in his office the head of an environmental protection foundation, who wants to hire someone and could she come in *right away*? "I told him you have a security problem that has nothing to do with loyalty. I told him you can write," the Section Chief says.

Miss X's search for a new job has been rather discouraging. She has allowed herself to become specialized and over-qualified. She has been on the verge of concealing her qualifications. She says yes, she will come in.

As it happens, Miss Y, assuming that Miss X would stay in all day, has worn the only good girdle to work. Miss X has not washed her hair. She cannot bear a shoe on her foot. And so when Miss X hastens to her job interview, she is quite "jiggly" of rear, greasy of hair, and wearing one shoe and one bunny slipper. She is hired. The Fish and Wildlife Service gives her a farewell party and a handsome gift — a lady's attaché case.

The Misses X and Y spent all their money moving *to* Washington and have none left to move *away* from it. They have a lease, the breaking of which costs them two months' rent.

They borrow from Miss X's future salary and move to New York. They rent an apartment on Bleecker Street in Greenwich Village. A little at a time they find friends of various orientations. When people in Miss X's office invite her to a party, they say, "Bring Miss Y." Then they turn to her male colleague and say, "And *your* wife's invited too, of course."

Sometimes Miss X grumbles and predicts that if the Government ever succeeds in rooting out all of its "security risks" it will find itself unable to govern. But usually she laughs and says that the "blankety-blank" security check was the best thing that ever happened to her. She really likes not lying.

I trust you can round it off in some artistic way, so the story *ends* instead of just *stopping*.

PAID UP

Emma's letter says, "My friend Valesca's starring in a play in New York. She's lonely and forlorn. How about giving her a call?" But Valesca is a medium-famous movie actress, so Lucille is scared to call her. Anyway, she and Vera haven't seen Valesca's play. Wouldn't she hate them for that? Tickets are seventeen dollars *each*, is why.

Still, when Emma's beautiful square blue envelope flies all the way from California to ask you to do something, you have to try. You have to rise above your natural backwardness and shyness and lack of worldly grace. You have to try.

There is a very shaky rumor, based on her

having worn a leather jacket once, that Valesca's a lesbian. "Is she?" Lucille asks the savvy new women from San Francisco.

"Are you kidding?" they sneer. "*Every*body knows that! She's slept with every woman west of the Mississippi."

So Lucille, who believes lesbians should all get to know each other and become a community, calls Valesca. She answers on the first ring. Lucille would know that voice anywhere. "Come see me. This afternoon," it commands.

Lucille wears her only dress, brown cotton, from Sears, trying to look respectable above Fourteenth Street. Valesca wears the first peignoir Lucille has ever seen, billowing pink, and pink satin high-heeled mules that make her lunge and stumble. Lucille sees with joy that Valesca is a klutz, like herself. Just a freckle-faced kid playing dress-up.

Valesca lives in the first penthouse Lucille has ever seen. There are flowering trees in tubs outside the windows. The living room is pink and cushiony and full of photographs of Valesca hugging famous people. Valesca says awful things about them, an easy flood of unembarrassed malice and bitchery and self-pity, no reserve, so indiscreet. How she trusts Lucille! They are already friends. Lucille is so flattered.

To celebrate the new friendship, Valesca breaks out champagne. They lap up glass after glass, and talk. Lucille says, "I live with a woman named Vera in the Village," and expects some hints in return. There is not one. Instead Valesca talks about all the Mr. Wrongs who present themselves disguised as Mr. Rights, and how disappointing that is.

Lucille's voice, inspired by Valesca's, becomes lush and round. She asks about Emma, who has never let Lucille meet her, even when the Navy stationed Lucille in California and she could have. When Lucille was nineteen she wrote Emma a fan letter about a book of hers that had a little indirect and negative lesbianism in it. Back then, you had to be a hero to say even that much and sign your real name. "I'm not very normal," Lucille told Emma. They've been writing to each other ever since, except for a fifteen-year gap while Lucille was married to Fred. "The boy who can't spell," Emma called him. Lucille shouldn't have told Emma that, but at the time it seemed kind of cute. After the divorce, living with Vera, Lucille wrote to Emma again. "I've been sick," she wrote. Emma answered, "We'd better stick together. We've got this uphill fight," and the blue envelopes started coming again.

Even so, Lucille doesn't know enough about Emma. She's never even seen a picture of her. Lucky Valesca has been in her very house.

"Tell me, tell me! Tell me about Emma!"

But Valesca is mostly interested in Emma's husband, wonderful Stanley. Lucille has pictured him blond, baldish, small, and pale. No! He is big, tanned, handsome, a real *man*, rancher and scholar and athlete, charming and witty, the poet on the football team, developed in every aspect, masses of glossy dark hair. There's nothing he can't do. With his own hands, he built a house for Emma. To Lucille, he sounds like a more polished version of Fred.

"And Emma?" Lucille asks.

Valesca sighs. Stanley adores Emma. He worships

her. It is one of the great unsolved mysteries of the universe, this undeserved devotion that never wavers, despite what that little bout with polio did to Emma, and that thing with her face, and now a breast gone too.

Lucille pictures poor bent, lopsided Emma dragging herself along, a pair of ragged claws with a permanent leer. Maybe the suicide attempt wrecked her face. That must be why she's never let Lucille see her. Lucille always thought it was because she loved Emma too much.

"Stanley carries Emma around on a cushion," Valesca says.

Lucille guesses Emma can't walk.

"Let's call them!" Valesca says. Not even waiting for night rates, she seizes the phone. She dials a ridiculously long number, endless, ten digits, without once speaking to an operator. How long has this been going on?

Emma's not home. Valesca talks with Stanley. The play, the rude audiences, the uncomprehending director, the faggot co-star who holds back from Valesca in the clinches, the noise, the dirt, the maids waking her up in the morning to clean, the building super coming in after the trash before she's dressed. Why will nobody understand that acting is *night work*?

Then she says, "I've got Lucille here. Want to talk with her?"

"Surely not!" Lucille says, but Valesca presses the phone into her hand.

"Poor man!" Lucille says, in a lush round hearty champagne voice. "You have to think of something to say to me."

"I've got plenty to say to you," Stanley says, very flatly.

"Oh?" Lucille says, staying warm, pretending she doesn't now realize, surprised, that he dislikes her. She braces herself for an attack that doesn't come. Stanley veers off. Uh, does Lucille know when Valesca's coming home? No, she doesn't, and here is Valesca. You can ask her face to face, so to speak.

Valesca calls Lucille every few days, sobbing, to say goodbye. She's going to step off the terrace. "Hold everything," Lucille says. "I'll be right there," and she jumps into her brown dress and listens again and again. The maids, the super, that faggot, the rude audiences, never getting to the top, always the bridesmaid, second-fiddle to all those fat horrid shot-full-of-hormones people.

She is spoiling Lucille's concentration on the book she's writing, but it is selfish to think of that when a friend's in trouble. Who's going to want Lucille's book anyway? She's not like Valesca. It's harder for Valesca to feel ugly and unsung than for Lucille to. Lucille's used to it, but Valesca expected to be a star.

Emma is coming to New York to get a prize. She'll be here a week. She'll stay at Valesca's, and go up to Nyack to see Carson McCullers, and curry favor with the prize people a little, but maybe see something of Lucille and Vera too, if that's okay.

Lucille writes back, yes, it's okay and then some. She writes, "There's something I want to tell you, that I think you don't know," and mails the letter fast before she can lose her nerve.

She wants to tell Emma about male lesbians — men who fall in love with lesbians. They are the best men you ever met, smart and full of feeling and good at their work. They don't drink or philander. They're not homosexual. You think maybe their health is contagious. You marry them in a big city or at a university, where there are lots of bright funny people, many of them lesbians, to be friends with, and before you know it you're living in some red-neck hamlet where, as Emma said of the place Stanley took her to, "If you walk downtown on Saturday night, you get tobacco juice on your legs," and the only friend you've got is your male lesbian. They are always hot for you, year after year. You can get fat and toothless and whiskery without deterring them. You can take to drink. Everybody wonders why they put up with you. They get you pregnant a lot, to keep you with them. They know you don't quite fully love them, but you do love your kids. They are wonderful fathers. You stay a long time, but not necessarily forever.

It seems wisest not to say this in a letter. Emma got mad when all Lucille said was, "Valesca says he carries you around on a cushion — or was it a plate?"

"Nobody gets carried around on anything around here," Emma answered. Being a genius at verbal expression, she made it blaze. "It's straight from the shoulder, right between the eyes, at all times, which is part of the fun opposite sexes can have, though some people haven't got the guts for it and prefer a Siamese twin."

So it seems best to wait until Emma's sitting right here, where the omens can be taken, to tell her that her wonderful Stanley has exploited her for thirty years. If she starts to get mad, Lucille can see it in time to back off.

How is Lucille to get ready for Emma? How handicapped is she? Should the bathroom have hand grips? Lucille is grateful now for this elevator building, which all of her and Vera's friends in their correct red-brick Village town houses pity and despise. At least it has no stairs. The hallway is bleak, but Lucille and Vera's apartment is nice, with windows looking north to the Empire State Building, which serves as a Christmas tree by night and a mountain by day. Somebody with a real mountain might find it dinky. Somebody from the spacious West might find the apartment dinky too, and wonder how much it costs, but unlike Vera's relatives not ask. ("You sure you Armenian?" they cry, on hearing how high the rent is.) Somebody in a wheelchair might get stuck in the living room between the couch and the walnut cabinet and Lucille's desk and Vera's electronic organ and the rocking chair and the dining table and chairs and the fish tank and the console-model phonograph. Somebody who's been to the Louvre might find the paintings, by untalented friends, naive to the point of pretentiousness, and might think there aren't that many books in the world worth keeping.

But nobody, Lucille swears, can find any dirt. She even calls the window cleaner.

Emma's call wakes Lucille early. Emma's at Kennedy Airport, and doesn't want to bother Valesca before three at the earliest. So where's Lucille's Bleecker Street anyway? Can a taxi find it?

Much too soon, Lucille is pacing the sidewalk in front of the building, like a lover. Will that celestial wheelchair never come?

"Lucille?" asks a small, symmetrical woman, rising healthily out of a cab unaided. In fact there's a spring in her step, though she is sixty-five and soon grappling with a huge suitcase. And her face looks good too, aging leanly into creases. A nice brown Western face, not a bit twisted.

Is there any way in which Valesca is not a malicious lying bitch?

And why hasn't Emma let Lucille see her all these years?

In the elevator, Emma says, "You're not so huge." Valesca must have told her Lucille is an elephant. "Just kinda corn-fed. Midwestern. Kinda wholesome. You look okay." This is an idea that doesn't come naturally to Lucille, but she smiles her thanks and Emma says, "Fluoridated. All those white teeth."

"You look okay too," Lucille says. "Are you hungry? Thirsty? Tired?"

"Naw."

"Want to sightsee?"

"Naw."

They sit at the table beside the clean windows

and look out across the Village rooftops instead of at each other.

Emma says, "The stuff you say, right out in letters."

"Well, that's the only way I have to tell you anything," Lucille says, hoping Emma won't notice the small reproach, but she does.

"You were too . . . overboard . . . about me. That's why I didn't let you come to the ranch."

"Yeah. I worked it out."

"I never ruined anybody that wasn't my own age. That's why I didn't come to the phone."

Emma has a writer's memory, equal to Lucille's own. She's talking about a call Lucille made twenty years ago from the bus station in Los Angeles. Emma's mother answered, flustered, like someone who doesn't lie much.

Lucille says, "You weren't home."

"No," Emma says, stuck in her old story.

Lucille says, "It's not that I had some great sexual passion for you."

Emma winces a little. Lucille doesn't know if "sexual" or "passion" did it. Or both.

Lucille says, "It's that here was this amazing wonderful woman I wanted to know."

"Aw shucks," Emma says. "This room has got the most stuff in it I ever saw. Stanley doesn't like you."

"I picked that up. And I hadn't even said that about carrying you on a plate yet."

"He says your voice is phony."

"Yeah. Valesca and I were drinking all afternoon, and I kept getting actressier and actressier and richer and yummier and velvet trombony. By the time she called you, I was awful."

103

"He says you proselytize. You advocate and foment."

"He's right. Our friends laugh at me. They say I think I died and went to heaven, so I want everybody to."

"He was all for you at first. Now he thinks you're a bad influence."

This is laughable. Lucille has never influenced anybody. She has a gift for arousing disagreement.

"Don't show him my letters?" she suggests.

"He brings in the mail."

"Could you get the mail?"

"Sometimes I do, and he says, 'What's in the mail?' and I say, 'Oh, this and that and so on, and a ... letter ... from ... Lucille —' "

"Lucille!" Lucille cries. "That bitch! That phony proselytizing bitch!"

Emma nods. "The enemy has struck again," she says.

Lucille says, "I used to let Fred read my mail because I got such good interesting funny letters that I was proud of, and I thought he'd enjoy them too, but he didn't. He just searched them for something to object to, and said, 'What did *you* say to make *her* say *this*?' "

"It's the same at our house."

"So I told him he couldn't read my mail anymore," Lucille says, hoping to be a bad influence.

"Just don't write so *much*, huh? You know what I hate?"

Lucille holds her breath. Which of her many indiscretions does Emma hate?

"I hate those damned nicknames, like Lefty and Blackie."

She means Lucille's dear butch friends Lefty and Blackie, whose adventures Lucille liked to tell her and can't again.

Emma says, "It's the shame of my life that I lived for three years with a woman named *Studs*."

Lucille hopes her laughter influences Emma to think maybe that wasn't so very shameful.

Emma says, "Then I went home to Stanley and my kids — to stay. That's God's way, my psychiatrists keep telling me."

When Lucille and Vera lasted past three years must have been the point where Lucille became a bad influence.

Emma says, "Before we got married, he offered me ... that. But it should be a nice woman and last a while. It should be serious. Nothing cheap or grubby. Nothing to harm the family."

"Nobody named Studs," Lucille says.

"You got it."

"It was okay with Fred too, but I couldn't find anybody. Once I almost did. I got two kisses. And Fred wanted to hear all about it, and like a damn fool I told him."

"Yeah."

"And then I couldn't keep him off me."

"Yeah."

"When all I wanted to do was stay alone and cry. Because like a damn fool, I told her I'd told him and it was okay with him. And away she went. Of course."

"Yeah."

"He thought he was comforting me. And I felt so guilty I let him."

"Yeah."

"We used to fall in love with the same woman, and she'd choose him. I mean, that happened once."

"Stanley and I did that too, but *I* won. I was always a charming kid."

"Valesca says Stanley's charming too."

"I guess so. For a while. All my psychiatrists have tried to get me to admit I hate him. But none of 'em could."

Lucille likes being influential. She likes it so much she laughs. Emma must see she has admitted she hates Stanley, because she instantly denies it. She says, "A man's better than a woman. A man goes out to work, but a woman's always around the house underfoot."

Lucille says, "Vera goes out to work, but Fred was always popping by — hoping to catch me at something. Isn't Stanley a farmer? They don't go away."

"We call it *rancher*. Oh, he lurks around outside a little."

"When Vera's hungry, she cooks. When Fred was hungry, he got white and faint and groaned that he was hypoglycemic, and you couldn't stall him with an apple or a piece of cheese. He wanted *food*. He wanted his *dinner*, damn it."

"Yeah. Stanley too. But it's my mother who cooks. I have to appreciate somebody who lets my mother live with me. They get along. Tired old veterans of me, rocking on the porch of the old soldiers' home. Talking it over. How awful it is or must be to be my husband or mother. He yells everything's her fault. I slept with her till I was nineteen."

"You did?" Lucille says, enviously. "I wanted to sleep with my mother but my father wouldn't let me."

"Yeah. But it's not recommended. The psychiatrists really home in on it. Pay dirt! And she's remorseful now. Stanley upbraids her and she does act of contrition upon act of contrition until he feels better."

"She has to stop saying she didn't *know,* and start saying, 'Lo, what a lowly worm am I!'"

"You got it."

"'Accept this humble chocolate cake, Cloud of Silence!'"

"He's getting fat," Emma says.

"Under the circumstances, he just about has to, with all that contrition."

"*In* the circumstances."

"Huh?"

"Stanley makes me say '*in* the circumstances.'"

"You tell Stanley that circumstances are a cloud we live under, not a ring we stand inside of," Lucille says, seeing but not admitting that *circum* means "around" and stances stand.

"Okay, I will," Emma says.

"Tell him I said so."

"I will. I had something with a girl once, who went on to get married and have a baby, and the baby was a Mongolian idiot. What's the euphemism these days? Downs syndrome? And I've always wondered whether that was my fault."

"You know it wasn't."

"Yeah. Did you ever hear of jet lag? I think I got it. You got a bed?"

Lucille takes her to the bedroom. It has a big bed for love and a little one for show, and chests and another million books.

"I thought the *living* room was full," Emma says.

In a minute she comes out, undressed to her slip. The scar where her left breast used to be shows.

"You got a shirt or something? I'm a little cold."

Lucille gives her an old soft faded-red sweatshirt of Vera's, saying, "You could get under the covers."

"Naw. That's too much," Emma says.

In a minute she comes out again. She sits in the rocking chair and looks at Lucille. The shirt or the bedroom has made her soft. She says, "I got a girl too. Name of Alice. She's a teacher. She's very shy. She's no good in any group that's got more than me in it. She's not pretty. But she's beautiful."

Lucille says, "I saw a picture of Eleanor Roosevelt the other day, and I thought, hey, that's the way to look. I finally saw her beauty."

"You got it," Emma says. "When I lost my breast was just about the best time I ever had, because Alice was with me every day in the hospital. But now I think — that stuff — is in the other breast too, and Alice can't be with me this time."

Lucille is weeping. "Why not? Why not?"

"Oh, you know. This and that."

"Stanley!"

"Yeah."

"Why doesn't he get a lover?"

"Listen, I'm not going to die or anything. It's okay. My family all live to be older than hell. My *mother's* still going strong. Speak up!"

Lucille, weeping, shakes her head.

"Alice really likes you. She's all for you. I keep

all your letters at her house. Listen, you can write all you want to. Send them there. Tell me about Lefty and Blackie. But don't say maybe I'm sick again. I don't want Alice to know that. Speak up, girl!"

Lucille shakes her head. Emma writes down Alice's address.

"Alice's house is so nice," Emma says. "I get all crazy at home and then every month or so I roar off down the highway to her house. I'm perfectly happy there. It's all white inside and out, except the floor's red tile, and the roof. She's got a yellow cat and a pink cat. I brought this on myself. I wouldn't take the testosterone anymore. I got all this facial hair, and Stanley would say, 'Use hirsute in a sentence,' and the kids would say, 'Her suit is too long.' Also I got too — uh — erotic. But I had something I could do about that. Alice didn't mind about the hair, either. She just loves me. Personally. Whatever happens. So I should have taken the damn hormone. But, you know, a girl's got her vanity. You've really got a home here. I didn't think that was possible in a big dumb jerrybuilt square thing. I should call Valesca. I like your furniture that you refinished. I like all your pictures except that one. You want me to live with Alice, don't you?"

"Yes."

"You're such a romantic. You're so impractical. Such a softie. I love this shirt."

"Please keep it."

"You mean it? Okay. Thanks. Stanley can't spell. Ah, that cheers you up."

Lucille laughs while still weeping. "But he's a poet," she says.

"Doesn't help."

"I guess it's in the blood," Lucille says.

Vera comes home early from work so she can meet Emma. Vera is short and plump, everybody's mama.

"I told Emma to keep your shirt," Lucille says.

"Good. Did you find out whether Valesca's a lesbian?"

Emma says, "I hate these damn labels. No, Valesca's not. And I'm not. Just because I love. Have loved for seventeen years. A woman. Doesn't make me. One of those."

Vera says, "Oh, I don't know. Labels are convenient. I'm an Armenian. I'm an economist. I'm a lesbian. Isn't that handier than saying I'm of Armenian descent, I have a degree in economics, and I love a woman?"

Lucille is very proud of Vera. She bets Studs never said anything that good. She bets there's no comparison.

Then, outdoing even her own self, Vera begins to talk about Emma's books, which she has read with intelligent care. She praises them in the way Lucille taught her, with examples. "I like it where they're shelling peas and humming," and so on, and Emma stays longer than she said she would, but does, in the end, really, have to get up to Valesca's. Valesca must already have little white cartons of Chinese food getting cold. She must be watching the news for plane crashes, because picturing you dead is how she shows affection.

Lucille walks with Emma toward Sheridan Square for a cab. In one hand she holds Emma's suitcase, in the other Emma's hand. Emma has put it there. Lucille would have been too shy, afraid Emma would mind holding hands on the street, even Christopher Street.

"I like your Vera," Emma says. "I didn't think I would. She sort of won me over. Make this last, will you? I'd like to see one last."

"I have every hope," Lucille says. "It looks somewhat possible. I think having been married helps. You can learn a little even there, about getting along."

"Yeah. It takes skill. Let nature take its course and it's over in five weeks. Unless one party just caves in, of course. I love your letters. Send them to Alice's."

"Why doesn't Stanley think *Alice* is a bad influence?"

"She doesn't advocate and foment. She just *does it*. Quietly."

"When I think of all the children growing up. Or grown up. With nobody to turn to. Nobody to tell. All the lonely years. Lifetimes, sometimes. Usually, maybe. All the lies we tell. And get told, about God's way and all that. When it could be so simple. Just love, but nobody will say a good word for it. I don't want to just do it quietly. I am disposed to advocate. Here's a cab." She thrusts up her hand like a bright student who knows the answer.

Emma says, "It's stopping! You're really urban! You've really got metropolitan know-how."

She gets into the cab. While the driver stows the suitcase, Emma rolls the window down. Lucille leans in. They press their cheeks together. "You're a good kid," Emma says. "No matter what anybody says about you, you fought for us in the war."

* * * * *

The phone rings while Vera and Lucille are at the very summit of lovemaking. They aren't going to answer, but then Lucille thinks maybe Emma is trying to reach her.

No. It is Valesca, asking is Emma there. Emma and Valesca disagreed about a couple of things, and Emma stormed out, and for all her fraudulent air of competence, Emma is a hick who doesn't know squat about cities. She's going to get herself murdered trying to hail a cab on Central Park West at midnight, or, God help her, riding the subway, and it will be Valesca's fault for years, when all she did was very nicely ask Emma to stop flaunting her damned scar and stop bad-mouthing poor Stanley, and anyway Emma didn't understand the play or how exhausting it is, just because Valesca makes it look easy, and where in hell *is* Emma? This is just typical of Emma. This is the crown and proof, if such were needed, of a long self-indulgent life as a spoiled brat, who has never let her mother go, whose children are crowding forty but she won't let them go, who rules mother and husband and children with a rod of iron, and if anybody resists *at all,* off she storms, off she roars into the night, but this time she won't get off so easy, not in New York.

And how is Lucille?

"Fine," Lucille says. "Emma's probably gone to a hotel."

"How's Vera?"

"Fine."

Vera has not heard Valesca's tirade so she is still up there, heaven or someplace.

Valesca says, "You sound funny. Vera's *not* all right. I can tell by your voice. She's real sick."

"No, she's fine."

"I can tell by your voice!"

"She's fine. She's better than fine. In fact, she's coming." Lucille shouldn't have said that, but she's not quite herself.

Valesca struggles in silence with the ambiguities of English, and then slams the phone down.

Lucille's rings again. Surely this time it is Emma.

"Hi," Emma says. "I can't tell you where I am." Does she think Lucille would bother her? "It's a hotel. It starts with A."

The Algonquin, Lucille thinks. Where else would a writer firmly stuck in the 1930s go?

Emma says, "If Valesca asks you, you don't know."

"In fact, I don't."

"That's why."

"Why did she want to hurt you when you're facing what you're facing? She is such a bitch."

"It's okay. That's just Valesca. She has a few quirks. I escaped. In one piece. Just in time. I'm fine. I accidentally brought away a knickknack she threw at me. It landed in my suitcase. She'll say I stole it. I'm going to spend tomorrow clearing my mind of all thought so I can give my speech and get my prize. Then I think maybe I'll just head back."

"Not go up to Nyack?"

"No. I think I'll go home."

"To Alice's?"

"I'll see how it goes. I'll let you know."

* * * * *

That seems to be the last of Emma, but she phones one more time, from the airport. "I told myself I could call if I remembered your number," she says. "And I did. What is it you want to tell me, that you think I don't know?"

"I shouldn't have said that," Lucille says, stumbling and flustered. "Anyway, you do know. It's between the lines in your books, I saw. Too late. After I said it. I take it all back."

Emma is firm. "What is it?" she asks.

"We already talked about it"

"What is it?"

"Uh, male lesbians. The men who fall in love with lesbians."

"So?"

"Well, they have, uh, traits, uh, in common."

"So?"

"That's all."

"So what do you do? Kick them in the teeth because they love you?"

"No. You just stop feeling so guilty. Like they're so healthy and you're so sick and you've ruined this wonderful man's life and all that. Because they've had a great time, and someday it gets to be your turn, because you're paid up. In full. That's all."

"Stanley did find somebody. He was packing to spend the weekend with her and I tried to shoot myself, but the damn gun wouldn't go off. He was fighting me for the gun, and the kids came in and caught us and laughed their heads off. They'd heard me suggest too many times, at the top of my voice, *find somebody else.* But when he did I felt so awful.

I sort of hang on over my own dead body. Like a turtle. Like a horse that keeps running back into the burning barn. It's not just him, you know. It's not that I don't need these psychiatrists. You're a good kid, but there's a lot you don't know."

"Yeah," Lucille says, feeling flawed as a writer for not knowing, but relieved as a person.

Emma says, "There's something about a promise. Or there used to be."

Lucille quotes Robert Browning: " 'You shouldn't take a boy of nine and make him promise not to like the girls.' "

"There's something about fighting it out year after year and coming through one more time, that sort of makes him your fate," Emma says.

"Remember what Colette's mother used to yell at Colette's father?"

"Not offhand."

" 'What are you to me? You are not my brother!' "

Emma says, "She was wrong. A husband can be your fate as much as a brother can."

The operator wants more money. Emma is out of coins. Lucille says, "Give me the number. I'll call you back."

"Naw. I'll write to you. Or Alice will," Emma says, and then there's a dial tone that Lucille listens to for a long time.

Alice does write, saying Emma wants Lucille to know she's come through the surgery fine but she's so queasy from radiation treatments that she can't say so herself.

Valesca phones to say goodbye. She's going to step off the terrace. *Good,* Lucille thinks, but says, to her shame, "Hold everything. I'll be right there." What a wimp!

Valesca is pacing in her tottery mules, sobbing, denouncing the maids, the super, that faggot, and now *this.* Hasn't Valesca suffered enough without *this*? Vera and Lucille! The two people in the world in whom it has been possible to imagine human decency, plain hick-town human decency!

"Oh, Lucille, how could you *do* this to me? I want you to know, I've been going to Saint Patrick's Cathedral every day to pray for you."

No two-bit parish church for Valesca, at least not when she's up against a sin of this magnitude. Now whenever Vera's not sexy, Lucille will think Valesca's prayers cured her.

"Tell me," Valesca says, burningly, "should I pray for Emma too?" Valesca will not turn away until she has an answer.

"I don't know," Lucille says.

"You do know. But you won't tell me. You people have this code of silence. Like the Mafia. I've been obsessed. Obsessed! Have I led Emma on over the years? Was it some twisted impulse of *love* that made her prefer death in the street to my rejection? When she flaunted her scar, was that an overture? And when I didn't respond, all her hopes collapsed and she had to flee? Is that it? Do you know?"

"No, I don't know," Lucille says. If she says she doubts it, will that reassure Valesca or insult her?

"How is she now?" Valesca asks, tender now toward the diseased heart she unwittingly broke. "Have you heard?"

"She's okay," Lucille says.

"I knew it!" Valesca cries, triumphant and bitter. "I knew it! It was all a big act."

"Well, there's more than one way to be okay. She lost her other breast."

Valesca covers her face with her hands, sobbing a horrible sob, unbearable grief. At last she is sorry, Lucille thinks. "Oh! Oh! Oh!" the famous voice groans from behind trembling hands. "Oh — poor — Stanley!"

"Poor *Stanley?*"

"All these years with his mother-in-law! And now a wife with no breasts!"

There is nothing to say, and no way to stay in this room. Lucille leaves without saying goodbye. Apparently Valesca does not step off the terrace. At least the *Times* doesn't say so.

Alice writes again. Emma is resting between a pink cat and a yellow one in a white bed in a white room in a white house. She wants Lucille to know she is completely happy. And in case Lucille is interested in someone she's never met, Alice takes this opportunity to say she too is completely happy.

BEGINNING

You say, "They show what becomes of people who have no spiritual life."

I say, "No spiritual life!"

"Irene said herself she's not a Christian. And certainly she's done things a Christian woman wouldn't be able to do. Most un-Christian women couldn't, for that matter."

You have not understood her. You have got hold of a few externals and shut your mind to all the rest.

I say, "You might equally think that because she was sustained by the great spiritual force of love, she was able to take a moral action that saved the lives and health and happiness and sanity of several people — her children, her ex-husband, his new wife, herself, Laura. How many's that? Eight?"

But my heart is out of the argument. I don't really hear you, your words. I hear only that my friends don't delight or move you, that you don't approve of me or them, that you wouldn't want for us a life like theirs. Well, I must be reasonable. I have spent six weeks refining and defining my feeling for you. Shall I call those six wasted weeks? What might I have spent them on instead? And haven't they been, often, blissful? Should I regret the hours I spent wondering what it meant that you caught my cold foot and warmed it in your hands?

From far away I hear you. Something about evil not being able to produce good, something about our having only Irene's own assertion that everything worked out well for everyone.

I say, "We have only her assertion for any of it. If she didn't say there'd been a divorce, we would have no way of knowing it. Believe one, believe the other. Is she a reliable reporter of her own life, or isn't she? To me she seems reliable."

"And those are your friends!"

"Yes!" I say. "And I think most people would honor them and honor me for having won their friendship."

It is done. There will be nothing. How can I live without your caress to imagine? In these six weeks, such dreams have become the breath of my life.

Can I claim you led me on? Yes and no. You piled hope on me with one hand but unloaded it with the other. I suppose what you put me in would come close to being literally a flap — back and forth, the winds of hope and despair. And now it will be only despair, my emotion a limp rag, broken balloon, sagging in one dull position.

The cab leaves us at my building. You pay the driver. I go up the steps and unlock the door. I wait. I am not certain you will come in. The cab drives off. You stand at the bottom of the steps. Perhaps you need an invitation. I can't speak. I hold the door invitingly as though I expect you. Awkwardly you climb the steps. Stumble. I am reminded of the many times I've stumbled in walking with you — how awkward one can be on feet numb with love and doubt. You are awkward. You are a big lady, tall, and fond of food. At her age, you will be a magnificent mountain like Irene. It's one more reason you should have liked her.

I thought we could make a long happy life. I thought it was hopeful that it's taken six weeks, which have made me love you more and more. I spoke to Irene of the time it was taking, as a good hopeful thing, and she said yes but not necessarily. She said that she had loved and waited for years and ended with nothing at all, not even a kiss after years of waiting love. So it can go that way too, she thought I should know. Now I will have to ask her whether not having had a kiss makes it easier afterward. I think it must. She told me once that it's harder to give up real children than imaginary ones. That was to suggest that I should know myself now and choose what I really am. And it's probably likewise easier to give up a fantasy kiss than a real one.

Well, so much for the Ouija board. I suppose Laura pushed it. It said, yes, you're gay. It said introducing you to them would precipitate our love, but it would be up to me to make the first move. In my fantasy I can easily approach and touch and hold and kiss you, but in life the Ouija statement is ridiculous. You are a scholar, you are tall, you are four years older than I, you pay the cab, you buy the theater tickets, you pick up the checks at dinner. It isn't possible that if you loved me you wouldn't be able to move towards me.

You sit on my couch. I used to plot how to get you there, keep you out of the chair, make you sit beside me. You go there now by yourself. "Drink?" I ask.

"No. Thanks. I can't stay." But you do stay.

"I'm sorry the evening was such a bust," I say.

"I knew we shouldn't on a Friday. The fish and everything. They didn't really respect that. And I doubt you did either. I resented, I must admit, the three of you sitting there boasting of the religions you've outgrown, so confident that in time I may mature to apostasy too."

"I don't think that was meany."

"Have you ever considered that I may not?" you say. "Do you ever seriously think that I may have found the true faith and that I may keep it? And that I may want friends who respect it? And that I may not want to share my life with someone who is just waiting for me to get over it?"

No, I haven't thought of that. But I think I won't say so. Could I become a Catholic for you? I don't know. Laura has made an occultist of Irene, but I doubt it was set up as a pre-condition.

"People who love begin to agree, I think," I say.

"I suppose your faith would influence whoever you lived with. Irene has taken up Laura's superstitions — says 'Bread and Butter,' like a child now."

"Catholicism is not a superstition."

"That was just an example. Why are you trying to pick a fight?"

You are quiet. I think I know why you want a fight — so we can make up. I say, "I think I'll have a drink."

"Then I will too."

I go to the kitchen. Make drinks. You stand in the doorway watching me, but as I come towards you, you fade back to the couch. I wish I knew what to do. I set the drinks on the coffee table.

I say, "I'm sorry you don't respect their life. It's what I'm looking for, I think."

"I didn't say I didn't respect it."

"Oh, I thought you did."

"It tempts me very much. Perhaps as an idea more than as a real thing. I could hope that even living such a life, I could still be a good Christian person and do some good in the world. They seem completely unaware of anything that doesn't relate to their own — peculiarity. I wouldn't want to be as narrow and cut off as that. I would want to live in an ordinary house in an ordinary city and move among ordinary people. They've made their own little false world as though the sexual function is all they define themselves by and all that interests them about other people."

"You misjudge them. They're interested in more things than anyone else I know. Economics, politics, art, history, architecture, music, the occult, psychology. When they take me walking in New York, I realize I've spent my life with my eyes shut."

"And yet they live in a homosexual neighborhood and devote the evening they first meet me to a discussion of what one would hope were intimate and painful revelations, which I have not requested, and I do not speak in kind."

"They were talking to me. They were assuming I'd told you about them, which I had."

"Where did you meet them?"

"Where? At their house. I was taken there by a friend."

"What friend?"

"Barbara."

"I've wondered what she is to you."

"Was."

"Was she?"

"Yes."

"How long?"

"A few months. Summer to summer. A year."

"What happened?"

"Intimate and painful revelations — haven't you just told me you disapprove of that kind of talk?"

"Only from those I've just met. Tell me. Why did it end with Barbara?"

"Many reasons. We never did get along. The last thing was that she wasn't ... faithful ... to me. So I left."

"Did she want you to stay?"

"She didn't want to fail again. In that way she wanted me to stay. It wasn't reason enough. I thought if I had to suffer anyway, I might as well have some of the positive things of life. Like children. Like money. Like a respectable home."

"Like marriage."

"Yes. That's what I thought. Suffering being my fate, a loveless life. Have those anyway. And there were plenty of men ready to oblige me. And no women to confuse me."

I stop. You know what comes next. One of us should say, "Until —" but neither of us does.

I say, "I talked with Irene and Laura about it. I thought Irene's life might be my guide. I might go her way. She's had it all — the whole range. Life can go that way. She proves it. But she doesn't recommend it. Even though some of us think it ended well for her."

"What does she recommend, as though I need ask?"

"I said nobody interested me. She said when I became internally ready someone would."

"Such as herself?"

What! You don't know anything or understand anything or deserve the evening they gave you or the weeks I kissed my pillow calling it by your name. I unname my pillow, I call back my love.

Oh, God, despair. Not to love you or hope for you or wait for you or plan for you or wonder what you mean and why you keep me waiting. There has been more pleasure in waiting for you than in embracing anyone else in my whole life. Not loving you brings back all the clouds and knots and griefs I ever fought against. I suffocate. I die. I would try to drink my drink but I think I would choke.

We sit side by side on my couch, which is my

bed. I am unable to speak, and for reasons of your own you don't either.

My cat jumps to your lap. You pet him although you don't like cats. Just tonight, at Irene and Laura's, you said, "Well, I like Tigger but that's because —" and then left the sentence for me to finish in my heart. Many times you've petted him on my lap and caught some of my leg or hand in the caress.

I watch your hands. Skillful, strong hands. Short nails, no ring, no polish. They are hands I dreamed would heal me. Tigger's hairs fall and cling to your dark slacks. It's wild to have a cat. I think I'll try to get Barbara to take him back. Hairs on my furniture, on my clothes, cat food in my refrigerator, Kitty Litter in my bathroom. It is mad. I think I will make my life very stripped and simple and get a lot of sleep.

You say, "I see I've made you angry."

"No. You just remind me that there is a reason, after all, why I spend twelve hundred dollars a year on a shrink. I was planning to give him up. I felt so well."

"My heart's just held together with a little spit and brown paper, too," you say. "Don't you see how scared I am?"

I reach out and lay my hand on Tigger's back. Your hands are very near and do not move away. Awkwardly and anxiously I capture one. You let it lie in my hand. I take courage to improve the relationship, to bring them palm to palm. Experience with men makes me afraid; so many times I have let my hand be taken and felt only boredom or oppression. I couldn't bear to make you feel such things. My sins of insincerity are coming home to roost.

I am not ready. I cannot immediately recover from the despair of so few minutes ago. Memory must guide me: until you spoke against my friends and the kind of love they symbolize, I longed for you. Somewhere inside I still must long for you. If you will receive me now, now is the time even though I have to go by memory. I remember many times that would have been better: the night we watched TV and you almost put your arm around me but then played with the ornament on the wall instead; the many nights you said you were leaving and then loitered against the door unable to go; the afternoon we got cold watching the skiing and you warmed my feet. If I had let you catch my eye any of those times, we would be already begun and not have this doubt and pain to go through.

Since it was I who held us back before, you leave it to me now. I have never done this, darling! I have only waited and let things happen.

Still holding your hand, I lean against your shoulder. Because you do not move, I trust that you don't object. But what a thing to trust in a woman! I turn my face. It is at the level of your neck, which is a good place to kiss you, so I kiss you there and you sigh and tilt your head back to give me your whole throat. The wonderful flow of power and possession and desire I feel at this sweet gesture makes me sure I can, after all, be the one who makes the moves and starts things. It is easy and natural now to get up on my knees and lean above your lifted face and take your glasses off and kiss your eyelids and face and mouth.

I feel a nervousness in you and I let your mouth go so you can tell me why. Your glasses worry you. What have I done with them? Have they fallen? Am I bending them? I say, "No, darling." I show them to you. "Look, not even smudged." But to ease you I put them on the table beside our evaporating drinks. We laugh. I like you very much. I say, "There's nothing the matter with either of us that a year or two of happiness won't fix."

You say, "This is terrible. I'm going to fall in love with you."

"You already have. It's all right. I won't hurt you."

"I'll just want to make love all the time."

"That's not terrible. That's nice."

"But I won't want to work and I won't get the good of my fellowship and it'll be awful."

"And I'll have to take care of you. I thought I was the baby and you were the grownup, but it's the opposite. You're a little lost child and you need me and I'm here and I love you."

Something in you draws back. Have I offended you? No. I think I have said something you've heard before. Jesus God, who do I look like? Who do I sound like? Does my kiss feel too much like somebody else's? Can't we have fifteen minutes without problems?

Gently I press your side to lay you down. You resist and then go. I lie against you, petting and kissing. Tigger leaps to the couch-back and watches. I'd like to be watching, too. I have never seen two women kiss. It must be nice to see. I wish movies showed it. They show other kinds of love. Why not ours?

I consider opening your shirt but you press so close that I think you don't want me to. It's all right. There's plenty of time. As many as sixty years maybe. Twenty-five plus sixty equals eight-five. Twenty-nine plus sixty equals eighty-nine. Quite possible, as healthy as we'll be once we get happy.

But you are crying. My cheek is wet with your tears. How bravely you cry, without a sound.

I say, "What is it, Angel?"

"I have to sit up. My nose is plugging."

I let you up. You sit very straight. Tigger jumps into your lap. I go to get you a Kleenex.

I say, "What is it, Baby?"

"I find. That. In my heart. I am. Married to someone else."

I wait.

"A girl. Woman. I knew at school. It was very hard for me. Because not natural, you know. And the Church has no sacrament for it. But I needed it. And maybe I rationalized or something — I came to feel that it was somehow a secret sacrament and no more unacceptable in the eyes of God than any other childless marriage. Because we didn't avoid children, we just couldn't have any. Through no choice of our own."

"Where is she now?" I ask.

"She's in Chicago."

"Chicago! Then you saw her last month."

"Yes. She said it's definitely over."

"Only last month!"

"Nothing's happened between us for two and a half years but I always felt it would again, you know?"

"But now you love me," I say. "It's all right. I

129

still loved Barbara until I began to love you. It always overlaps. You can't expect to stop until you have someone else. That's why you went there, to be divorced, so you could love me. And now you do."

"That's not the point. She can divorce me, but I find I can't remarry."

I shake my head and reach for my drink. It is mostly melted ice, but it helps. It keeps me from saying this is a conversation too surrealistic to keep track of. It keeps me from saying, well, nobody can say you're one of these no-good, reckless, irresponsible, amoral modern kids. I feel many such unwise thoughts crowding to be said.

"Can you have a roll in the hay?" I ask. I might as well have said the other. Before I can hurt you more, I go to the bathroom and wash my face and breathe awhile and comb my hair.

When I come back, you have your coat on. "I'll phone you," you say.

"All right."

You have never got away so fast before. You are in the hall when the panic hits me. I run to the door and call your name. You come back. I kick the door shut and stumble into your arms. Your big body enfolds me. You kiss me a long aching goodbye, but afterwards you still say, "I'll call you."

It is morning. I haven't slept. I wait for it to be late enough to call Irene and Laura. They are my mothers and will comfort me and tell me everything will be all right and that I will soon be happy. At ten I can wait no longer. Irene answers, not crossly but strangling with sleep. I choke and say nothing and hang up. Ten o'clock on Saturday morning is too early to call even the fire department.

So I call the shrink at his home in Connecticut. This I may do because I pay him twelve hundred dollars a year to be there for me to lean on. He too is sleeping but I think of the money and have no pity. I am crying, I find. He makes me very young. I curry favor by explaining how right he was. Yes, this with a woman is such a bad idea, so enfeebling, so backward-moving, so unsound, so masochistic and self-defeating and dead-end. "You'd better come up," he says.

I am to go to his house and we'll talk it over. He'll meet me at the station. I suppose I am to see a healthy household and be given a pill and watched. A good enough way to spend a Saturday I have no possible use for.

From Penn Station I phone Irene and Laura again. Irene answers, still asleep, although it is now eleven. But since I can be no other inconvenience all day, I am bold and speak. Her voice brightens. She calls me dear. (She would have done the same at ten!) I say, "I'm on my way to Connecticut. I had to be the one to start it."

"Then it has started — how good," she says.

I say, "Well, there are problems. What's the noise in the phone?"

"Pay phones always do this. It's nothing."

"What did you think of her?" I ask.

"Well, I"m not a quick judge. I liked her. I felt she's someone who doesn't have to have everything her own way — who can discuss. And any problem you can discuss you can get somewhere on."

"You think so?" I say. Oh, poor Irene, liking you and being judged by the Spanish Inquisition in return!

She says, "I regret I yattered so much. I was so curious about her I was afraid I'd try to pump her if I didn't yatter." Non-Christians have morals you wouldn't understand.

I say, "What's the clicking in the phone?"

"It's signaling the operator to make her ask you for a nickel."

"I have to go. I can't talk on this phone."

"How long will you be gone?"

"Till Monday morning," I say and wonder where that came from. Yes, it is what I want her to tell you if you ask her where I am.

"Call us when you get back, please." Her voice is loving and concerned. She would have been this way at ten.

But the train is a good enough place to be. I get glimpses of the Sound. I need the sight of water. I need to walk and get very tired and think. I need to decide how many more times I can let a woman break my heart before it breaks beyond repair.

I will rent a hotel room in Connecticut and walk and get very tired and not come back until Monday. I want you to ring and ring my phone and lurk at my door. If you ask Irene and Laura where I am, I will know there's hope for you and me.

THE NIGHT THE CURSE
WAS BLESSED

We had a lovely night of holding and touching and remembering. When I got up to pee, I found I had the curse and went back and told Fern.

I said, "The only time you ever whined with me was once when you came back to bed to say you had the curse and cramps."

She said, "It was awful of me to whine and show you I am capable of whining."

I said, "No, it wasn't."

She said when she first heard of menstruation she questioned her parents intensively to find out about a comparable handicap men have. She found none and felt indignant and abused, put-upon. She said she might not have become a lesbian except for that injustice. And I felt such gratitude to menstruation for making her a lesbian that I felt tempted to say nothing against it.

But then I admitted that once, at the beginning, I forgot a used Kotex in the bathroom and my brother found it and reproached me, and I felt very grubby and, yes, put-upon. And Fern hugged me and wanted to take that away from me.

I said that once I bled all over some pajamas and didn't know what to do — didn't want my brother to find them soaking — and I put them into a big tin can to soak and put it into the upstairs hall closet and forgot it. Next time I found it, it was rusty and stinky and I didn't know what to do so I left it there, and my mother found it and washed the pajamas and *said nothing*. I began to weep telling Fern how my mother understood and said *nothing* and solved the problem I was unable to solve, and how grateful I've always been that she *said nothing*.

Fern said we were too hot and should take one of the quilts off. "You're sweating. I feel it on your temples," she said.

I said, "Them's tears."

She hugged me even closer and said, "How could I not know?"

I said, "Because I'm so good at it. Don't mind, because my poor old Mama died and I didn't cry much then, and it's good for me to come upon memories that help me cry for her."

And Fern held me so warm and close and good,

trying to take away from me the pain of being a woman, and my mother's pain also, I think.

ON ADDING A CUBIT

You're supposed to clasp a sled like a lover, press it
    against you and run with it and fling yourself
    forward, *slam!*
My brother Dick could do that, but I couldn't. I was
    afraid, and that's the basic natural type I am.
He could also jump off the barn beam and catch a
    rope and swing on it to the beam on the other
    side.
Needless to say, I couldn't. But the surprise is, after
    taking thought, I could, and when my turn was
    delayed I cried.
I was a good sled-slammer before I went on to
    higher things, too.
And climbed up and stood on the smokestack of the
    Traverse City Socony (a Great Lakes tanker,
    good-sized), though scared of heights, and looked
    around at the view. (Blue to the horizon, blue.)
I'm trying to say, it takes more than one whimper to
    make a coward, or don't despair of me, my record
    is sound.
Though I may shake right now, nothing final is
    meant. Taking thought will bring me around.

SARAH, EAVESDROPPING

Sarah, eavesdropping in her tent,
overheard the angel say
she'd have — at her age! —
a son, and smiled.

I saw that smile the other night
when I kissed you
and your face went East.
The West fell off you
like a leaf
right in my hands,
and there were all the goddesses —
Rachel, Rebecca, Sarah, Judith, Ruth —
or is she only one with many names?
Christians get canonized if once,
as Mary, she lets them even see her,
and there was I with my lips on her.
I may never be humble again.

You said your name is really Bathsheba,
and smiled, and I knew
you'd heard the angel say
we'd have — at our age! — love,
and what do angels know?

THE PROMISE

When there was no more busy-work to do,
I leaned across the couch arm
and laid my lips against your hair.
You raised your face. I said,
"Don't be afraid. I'll always love you.
It can't get worse." "I didn't forget,"
you said. "How could you think I did?"
So we began again.

Our heaven, second series.

You heal the inborn isolation of my life.

We've learned a little.
I hope we've learned
to live without security.
We always did know not to promise.

But, Nath, tonight
when I don't know
(and maybe even you don't)
what will be in your face tomorrow,
I feel "Don't be afraid"
was a promise not to suffer.
This is to say
I remember and will do my best.

THE OLD CROWD

They look the same except that Andy's forehead
is half his head. Both handsome, slender, vital.
Later I said, "Sloan never ages — still looks like a
　　boy."
"A boy of what age?" Julie asked. I whimpered,
　　"Thirty?"
"More like fifty," Julie said.

They don't know what to do with all their money.
"Give it to SAGE," I said. "They're making us a
　　place."
"No, we won't wait for that."
I said, "We all imagine we'll crawl off
like Eskimos, but then the time comes and we don't.
The Eskimos don't either, till they get worn down
by all the hints."

They said Claudette had cancer, lost a lot of organs,
is very thin and tense. Sal has grown tiny. Her
　　neck's
inside her shoulders. Bill and Victor
broke up when Bill (I thought it would be Victor)
turned crotchety and crazy, mean. He moved
back home to Texas, lives in somebody's garage.

All this bad news seems merely interesting.
Yes, I'm relieved. The years that made me old
have been busy elsewhere too.

A few of the publications of
THE NAIAD PRESS, INC.
P.O. Box 10543 • Tallahassee, Florida 32302
Phone (904) 539-5965
Mail orders welcome. Please include 15% postage.

A DOORYARD FULL OF FLOWERS by Isabel Miller. 160 pp.
Stories incl. 2 sequels to *Patience and Sarah.*   ISBN 1-56280-029-9 $9.95

MURDER BY TRADITION by Katherine V. Forrest. 288 pp. A
Kate Delafield Mystery. 4th in a series.   (HC) ISBN 0-941483-89-4   18.95
                                        (Paperback) ISBN 1-56280-002-7   9.95

THE EROTIC NAIAD edited by Katherine V. Forrest & Barbara Grier.
224 pp. Love stories by Naiad Press authors.   ISBN 1-56280-026-4   12.95

DEAD CERTAIN by Claire McNab. 224 pp. 5th Det. Insp. Carol
Ashton mystery.   ISBN 1-56280-027-2   9.95

CRAZY FOR LOVING by Jaye Maiman. 320 pp. 2nd Robin
Miller mystery.   ISBN 1-56280-025-6   9.95

STONEHURST by Barbara Johnson. 176 pp. Passionate regency
romance.   ISBN 1-56280-024-8   9.95

INTRODUCING AMANDA VALENTINE by Rose Beecham.
256 pp. An Amanda Valentine Mystery — 1st in a series.
                                    ISBN 1-56280-021-3   9.95

UNCERTAIN COMPANIONS by Robbi Sommers. 204 pp.
Steamy, erotic novel.   ISBN 1-56280-017-5   9.95

A TIGER'S HEART by Lauren W. Douglas. 240 pp. Fourth Caitlin
Reece Mystery.   ISBN 1-56280-018-3   9.95

PAPERBACK ROMANCE by Karin Kallmaker. 256 pp. A
delicious romance.   ISBN 1-56280-019-1   9.95

MORTON RIVER VALLEY by Lee Lynch. 304 pp. Lee Lynch at
her best!   ISBN 1-56280-016-7   9.95

LOVE, ZENA BETH by Diane Salvatore. 224 pp. The most talked
about lesbian novel of the nineties!   ISBN 1-56280-015-9   18.95

THE LAVENDER HOUSE MURDER by Nikki Baker. 224 pp. A
Virginia Kelly Mystery. Second in a series.   ISBN 1-56280-012-4   9.95

PASSION BAY by Jennifer Fulton. 224 pp. Passionate romance,
virgin beaches, tropical skies.   ISBN 1-56280-028-0   9.95

STICKS AND STONES by Jackie Calhoun. 208 pp. Contemporary
lesbian lives and loves.   ISBN 1-56280-020-5   9.95

DELIA IRONFOOT by Jeane Harris. 192 pp. Adventure for Delia
and Beth in the Utah mountains.   ISBN 1-56280-014-0   9.95

UNDER THE SOUTHERN CROSS by Claire McNab. 192 pp.
Romantic nights Down Under.   ISBN 1-56280-011-6   9.95

RIVERFINGER WOMEN by Elana Nachman/Dykewomon.
208 pp. Classic Lesbian/feminist novel.   ISBN 1-56280-013-2   8.95

A CERTAIN DISCONTENT by Cleve Boutell. 240 pp. A unique
coterie of women.   ISBN 1-56280-009-4   9.95

GRASSY FLATS by Penny Hayes. 256 pp. Lesbian romance in
the '30s.   ISBN 1-56280-010-8   9.95

A SINGULAR SPY by Amanda K. Williams. 192 pp. 3rd spy novel
featuring Lesbian agent Madison McGuire.   ISBN 1-56280-008-6   8.95

THE END OF APRIL by Penny Sumner. 240 pp. A Victoria Cross
Mystery. First in a series.   ISBN 1-56280-007-8   8.95

A FLIGHT OF ANGELS by Sarah Aldridge. 240 pp. Romance set at
the National Gallery of Art   ISBN 1-56280-001-9   9.95

HOUSTON TOWN by Deborah Powell. 208 pp. A Hollis Carpenter
mystery. Second in a series.   ISBN 1-56280-006-X   8.95

KISS AND TELL by Robbi Sommers. 192 pp. Scorching stories by
the author of *Pleasures*.   ISBN 1-56280-005-1   9.95

STILL WATERS by Pat Welch. 208 pp. Second in the Helen
Black mystery series.   ISBN 0-941483-97-5   9.95

MURDER IS GERMANE by Karen Saum. 224 pp. The 2nd
Brigid Donovan mystery.   ISBN 0-941483-98-3   8.95

TO LOVE AGAIN by Evelyn Kennedy. 208 pp. Wildly
romantic love story.   ISBN 0-941483-85-1   9.95

IN THE GAME by Nikki Baker. 192 pp. A Virginia Kelly
mystery. First in a series.   ISBN 01-56280-004-3   9.95

AVALON by Mary Jane Jones. 256 pp. A Lesbian Arthurian
romance.   ISBN 0-941483-96-7   9.95

STRANDED by Camarin Grae. 320 pp. Entertaining, riveting
adventure.   ISBN 0-941483-99-1   9.95

THE DAUGHTERS OF ARTEMIS by Lauren Wright Douglas.
240 pp. Third Caitlin Reece mystery.   ISBN 0-941483-95-9   9.95

CLEARWATER by Catherine Ennis. 176 pp. Romantic secrets
of a small Louisiana town.   ISBN 0-941483-65-7   8.95

THE HALLELUJAH MURDERS by Dorothy Tell. 176 pp.
Second Poppy Dillworth mystery.   ISBN 0-941483-88-6   8.95

ZETA BASE by Judith Alguire. 208 pp. Lesbian triangle
on a future Earth.   ISBN 0-941483-94-0   9.95

SECOND CHANCE by Jackie Calhoun. 256 pp. Contemporary
Lesbian lives and loves.   ISBN 0-941483-93-2   9.95

BENEDICTION by Diane Salvatore. 272 pp. Striking,
contemporary romantic novel.   ISBN 0-941483-90-8   9.95

CALLING RAIN by Karen Marie Christa Minns. 240 pp.
Spellbinding, erotic love story   ISBN 0-941483-87-8   9.95

BLACK IRIS by Jeane Harris. 192 pp. Caroline's hidden past . . .
                                                   ISBN 0-941483-68-1   8.95

TOUCHWOOD by Karin Kallmaker. 240 pp. Loving, May/
December romance.   ISBN 0-941483-76-2   9.95

BAYOU CITY SECRETS by Deborah Powell. 224 pp. A Hollis
Carpenter mystery. First in a series.   ISBN 0-941483-91-6   9.95

COP OUT by Claire McNab. 208 pp. 4th Det. Insp. Carol Ashton
mystery.   ISBN 0-941483-84-3   9.95

LODESTAR by Phyllis Horn. 224 pp. Romantic, fast-moving
adventure.   ISBN 0-941483-83-5   8.95

THE BEVERLY MALIBU by Katherine V. Forrest. 288 pp. A
Kate Delafield Mystery. 3rd in a series. (HC)   ISBN 0-941483-47-9   16.95
                             Paperback   ISBN 0-941483-48-7   9.95

THAT OLD STUDEBAKER by Lee Lynch. 272 pp. Andy's affair
with Regina and her attachment to her beloved car.
                                                   ISBN 0-941483-82-7   9.95

PASSION'S LEGACY by Lori Paige. 224 pp. Sarah is swept into
the arms of Augusta Pym in this delightful historical romance.
                                                   ISBN 0-941483-81-9   8.95

THE PROVIDENCE FILE by Amanda Kyle Williams. 256 pp.
Second espionage thriller featuring lesbian agent Madison McGuire
                                                   ISBN 0-941483-92-4   8.95

I LEFT MY HEART by Jaye Maiman. 320 pp. A Robin Miller
Mystery. First in a series.   ISBN 0-941483-72-X   9.95

THE PRICE OF SALT by Patricia Highsmith (writing as Claire
Morgan). 288 pp. Classic lesbian novel, first issued in 1952 . . .
acknowledged by its author under her own, very famous, name.
                                                   ISBN 1-56280-003-5   9.95

SIDE BY SIDE by Isabel Miller. 256 pp. From beloved author of
Patience and Sarah.   ISBN 0-941483-77-0   9.95

SOUTHBOUND by Sheila Ortiz Taylor. 240 pp. Hilarious sequel
to *Faultline.*   ISBN 0-941483-78-9   8.95

STAYING POWER: LONG TERM LESBIAN COUPLES
by Susan E. Johnson. 352 pp. Joys of coupledom.
                                                   ISBN 0-941-483-75-4   12.95

SLICK by Camarin Grae. 304 pp. Exotic, erotic adventure.
                                                   ISBN 0-941483-74-6   9.95

NINTH LIFE by Lauren Wright Douglas. 256 pp. A Caitlin
Reece mystery. 2nd in a series.   ISBN 0-941483-50-9   8.95

PLAYERS by Robbi Sommers. 192 pp. Sizzling, erotic novel.
                                                   ISBN 0-941483-73-8   9.95

MURDER AT RED ROOK RANCH by Dorothy Tell. 224 pp.
First Poppy Dillworth adventure. ISBN 0-941483-80-0 8.95

LESBIAN SURVIVAL MANUAL by Rhonda Dicksion.
112 pp. Cartoons! ISBN 0-941483-71-1 8.95

A ROOM FULL OF WOMEN by Elisabeth Nonas. 256 pp.
Contemporary Lesbian lives. ISBN 0-941483-69-X 9.95

MURDER IS RELATIVE by Karen Saum. 256 pp. The first
Brigid Donovan mystery. ISBN 0-941483-70-3 8.95

PRIORITIES by Lynda Lyons 288 pp. Science fiction with
a twist. ISBN 0-941483-66-5 8.95

THEME FOR DIVERSE INSTRUMENTS by Jane Rule. 208
pp. Powerful romantic lesbian stories. ISBN 0-941483-63-0 8.95

LESBIAN QUERIES by Hertz & Ertman. 112 pp. The questions
you were too embarrassed to ask. ISBN 0-941483-67-3 8.95

CLUB 12 by Amanda Kyle Williams. 288 pp. Espionage thriller
featuring a lesbian agent! ISBN 0-941483-64-9 8.95

DEATH DOWN UNDER by Claire McNab. 240 pp. 3rd Det.
Insp. Carol Ashton mystery. ISBN 0-941483-39-8 9.95

MONTANA FEATHERS by Penny Hayes. 256 pp. Vivian and
Elizabeth find love in frontier Montana. ISBN 0-941483-61-4 8.95

CHESAPEAKE PROJECT by Phyllis Horn. 304 pp. Jessie &
Meredith in perilous adventure. ISBN 0-941483-58-4 8.95

LIFESTYLES by Jackie Calhoun. 224 pp. Contemporary Lesbian
lives and loves. ISBN 0-941483-57-6 9.95

VIRAGO by Karen Marie Christa Minns. 208 pp. Darsen has
chosen Ginny. ISBN 0-941483-56-8 8.95

WILDERNESS TREK by Dorothy Tell. 192 pp. Six women on
vacation learning "new" skills. ISBN 0-941483-60-6 8.95

MURDER BY THE BOOK by Pat Welch. 256 pp. A Helen
Black Mystery. First in a series. ISBN 0-941483-59-2 9.95

BERRIGAN by Vicki P. McConnell. 176 pp. Youthful Lesbian —
romantic, idealistic Berrigan. ISBN 0-941483-55-X 8.95

LESBIANS IN GERMANY by Lillian Faderman & B. Eriksson.
128 pp. Fiction, poetry, essays. ISBN 0-941483-62-2 8.95

THERE'S SOMETHING I'VE BEEN MEANING TO TELL
YOU Ed. by Loralee MacPike. 288 pp. Gay men and lesbians
coming out to their children. ISBN 0-941483-44-4 9.95
 ISBN 0-941483-54-1 16.95

LIFTING BELLY by Gertrude Stein. Ed. by Rebecca Mark. 104
pp. Erotic poetry. ISBN 0-941483-51-7 8.95
 ISBN 0-941483-53-3 14.95

ROSE PENSKI by Roz Perry. 192 pp. Adult lovers in a long-term
relationship.   ISBN 0-941483-37-1   8.95

AFTER THE FIRE by Jane Rule. 256 pp. Warm, human novel
by this incomparable author.   ISBN 0-941483-45-2   8.95

SUE SLATE, PRIVATE EYE by Lee Lynch. 176 pp. The gay
folk of Peacock Alley are *all cats*.   ISBN 0-941483-52-5   8.95

CHRIS by Randy Salem. 224 pp. Golden oldie. Handsome Chris
and her adventures.   ISBN 0-941483-42-8   8.95

THREE WOMEN by March Hastings. 232 pp. Golden oldie. A
triangle among wealthy sophisticates.   ISBN 0-941483-43-6   8.95

RICE AND BEANS by Valeria Taylor. 232 pp. Love and
romance on poverty row.   ISBN 0-941483-41-X   8.95

PLEASURES by Robbi Sommers. 204 pp. Unprecedented
eroticism.   ISBN 0-941483-49-5   8.95

EDGEWISE by Camarin Grae. 372 pp. Spellbinding
adventure.   ISBN 0-941483-19-3   9.95

FATAL REUNION by Claire McNab. 224 pp. 2nd Det. Inspec.
Carol Ashton mystery.   ISBN 0-941483-40-1   8.95

KEEP TO ME STRANGER by Sarah Aldridge. 372 pp. Romance
set in a department store dynasty.   ISBN 0-941483-38-X   9.95

HEARTSCAPE by Sue Gambill. 204 pp. American lesbian in
Portugal.   ISBN 0-941483-33-9   8.95

IN THE BLOOD by Lauren Wright Douglas. 252 pp. Lesbian
science fiction adventure fantasy   ISBN 0-941483-22-3   8.95

THE BEE'S KISS by Shirley Verel. 216 pp. Delicate, delicious
romance.   ISBN 0-941483-36-3   8.95

RAGING MOTHER MOUNTAIN by Pat Emmerson. 264 pp.
Furosa Firechild's adventures in Wonderland.   ISBN 0-941483-35-5   8.95

IN EVERY PORT by Karin Kallmaker. 228 pp. Jessica's sexy,
adventuresome travels.   ISBN 0-941483-37-7   9.95

OF LOVE AND GLORY by Evelyn Kennedy. 192 pp. Exciting
WWII romance.   ISBN 0-941483-32-0   8.95

CLICKING STONES by Nancy Tyler Glenn. 288 pp. Love
transcending time.   ISBN 0-941483-31-2   9.95

SURVIVING SISTERS by Gail Pass. 252 pp. Powerful love
story.   ISBN 0-941483-16-9   8.95

SOUTH OF THE LINE by Catherine Ennis. 216 pp. Civil War
adventure.   ISBN 0-941483-29-0   8.95

WOMAN PLUS WOMAN by Dolores Klaich. 300 pp. Supurb
Lesbian overview.   ISBN 0-941483-28-2   9.95

SLOW DANCING AT MISS POLLY'S by Sheila Ortiz Taylor.
96 pp. Lesbian Poetry   ISBN 0-941483-30-4   7.95

DOUBLE DAUGHTER by Vicki P. McConnell. 216 pp. A Nyla
Wade Mystery, third in the series.   ISBN 0-941483-26-6   8.95

HEAVY GILT by Delores Klaich. 192 pp. Lesbian detective/
disappearing homophobes/upper class gay society.
                                            ISBN 0-941483-25-8   8.95

THE FINER GRAIN by Denise Ohio. 216 pp. Brilliant young
college lesbian novel.   ISBN 0-941483-11-8   8.95

THE AMAZON TRAIL by Lee Lynch. 216 pp. Life, travel & lore
of famous lesbian author.   ISBN 0-941483-27-4   8.95

HIGH CONTRAST by Jessie Lattimore. 264 pp. Women of the
Crystal Palace.   ISBN 0-941483-17-7   8.95

OCTOBER OBSESSION by Meredith More. Josie's rich, secret
Lesbian life.   ISBN 0-941483-18-5   8.95

LESBIAN CROSSROADS by Ruth Baetz. 276 pp. Contemporary
Lesbian lives.   ISBN 0-941483-21-5   9.95

BEFORE STONEWALL: THE MAKING OF A GAY AND
LESBIAN COMMUNITY by Andrea Weiss & Greta Schiller.
96 pp., 25 illus.   ISBN 0-941483-20-7   7.95

WE WALK THE BACK OF THE TIGER by Patricia A. Murphy.
192 pp. Romantic Lesbian novel/beginning women's movement.
                                            ISBN 0-941483-13-4   8.95

SUNDAY'S CHILD by Joyce Bright. 216 pp. Lesbian athletics, at
last the novel about sports.   ISBN 0-941483-12-6   8.95

OSTEN'S BAY by Zenobia N. Vole. 204 pp. Sizzling adventure
romance set on Bonaire.   ISBN 0-941483-15-0   8.95

LESSONS IN MURDER by Claire McNab. 216 pp. 1st Det. Inspec.
Carol Ashton mystery — erotic tension!.   ISBN 0-941483-14-2   8.95

YELLOWTHROAT by Penny Hayes. 240 pp. Margarita, bandit,
kidnaps Julia.   ISBN 0-941483-10-X   8.95

SAPPHISTRY: THE BOOK OF LESBIAN SEXUALITY by
Pat Califia. 3d edition, revised. 208 pp.   ISBN 0-941483-24-X   8.95

CHERISHED LOVE by Evelyn Kennedy. 192 pp. Erotic
Lesbian love story.   ISBN 0-941483-08-8   9.95

LAST SEPTEMBER by Helen R. Hull. 208 pp. Six stories & a
glorious novella.   ISBN 0-941483-09-6   8.95

THE SECRET IN THE BIRD by Camarin Grae. 312 pp. Striking,
psychological suspense novel.   ISBN 0-941483-05-3   8.95

TO THE LIGHTNING by Catherine Ennis. 208 pp. Romantic
Lesbian 'Robinson Crusoe' adventure.   ISBN 0-941483-06-1   8.95

THE OTHER SIDE OF VENUS by Shirley Verel. 224 pp.
Luminous, romantic love story.   ISBN 0-941483-07-X   8.95

DREAMS AND SWORDS by Katherine V. Forrest. 192 pp.
Romantic, erotic, imaginative stories.   ISBN 0-941483-03-7   8.95

MEMORY BOARD by Jane Rule. 336 pp. Memorable novel
about an aging Lesbian couple.   ISBN 0-941483-02-9   9.95

THE ALWAYS ANONYMOUS BEAST by Lauren Wright
Douglas. 224 pp. A Caitlin Reece mystery. First in a series.
                                       ISBN 0-941483-04-5   8.95

SEARCHING FOR SPRING by Patricia A. Murphy. 224 pp.
Novel about the recovery of love.   ISBN 0-941483-00-2   8.95

DUSTY'S QUEEN OF HEARTS DINER by Lee Lynch. 240 pp.
Romantic blue-collar novel.   ISBN 0-941483-01-0   8.95

PARENTS MATTER by Ann Muller. 240 pp. Parents'·
relationships with Lesbian daughters and gay sons.
                                       ISBN 0-930044-91-6   9.95

THE PEARLS by Shelley Smith. 176 pp. Passion and fun in
the Caribbean sun.   ISBN 0-930044-93-2   7.95

MAGDALENA by Sarah Aldridge. 352 pp. Epic Lesbian novel
set on three continents.   ISBN 0-930044-99-1   8.95

THE BLACK AND WHITE OF IT by Ann Allen Shockley.
144 pp. Short stories.   ISBN 0-930044-96-7   7.95

SAY JESUS AND COME TO ME by Ann Allen Shockley. 288
pp. Contemporary romance.   ISBN 0-930044-98-3   8.95

LOVING HER by Ann Allen Shockley. 192 pp. Romantic love
story.   ISBN 0-930044-97-5   7.95

MURDER AT THE NIGHTWOOD BAR by Katherine V.
Forrest. 240 pp. A Kate Delafield mystery. Second in a series.
                                       ISBN 0-930044-92-4   9.95

ZOE'S BOOK by Gail Pass. 224 pp. Passionate, obsessive love
story.   ISBN 0-930044-95-9   7.95

WINGED DANCER by Camarin Grae. 228 pp. Erotic Lesbian
adventure story.   ISBN 0-930044-88-6   8.95

PAZ by Camarin Grae. 336 pp. Romantic Lesbian adventurer
with the power to change the world.   ISBN 0-930044-89-4   8.95

SOUL SNATCHER by Camarin Grae. 224 pp. A puzzle, an
adventure, a mystery — Lesbian romance.   ISBN 0-930044-90-8   8.95

These are just a few of the many Naiad Press titles — we are the oldest and
largest lesbian/feminist publishing company in the world. Please request a
complete catalog. We offer personal service; we encourage and welcome direct
mail orders from individuals who have limited access to bookstores carrying
our publications.